Is it just music...or love?

"I keep thinking about Don Stanton," Karen said with a smile. "Did I tell you he gave me a ride home from school yesterday?"

"No, you didn't. Tell me everything!"

Gwen listened excitedly as Karen told her about Don's interest in setting Karen's lyrics to music. He was, after all, Hampstead High's top rock musician.

"Didn't I tell you you'd make beautiful music together?" Gwen exclaimed when Karen had finished. "Wow—now you've got *two* good-looking, eligible guys interested in you at the same time! Unbelievable!" Gwen let out a long sigh.

"Hold on, Gwen. No one said Don was interested in me. It's my lyrics he's after." But deep down, Karen hoped her friend was right...

HAMPSTEAD HIGH

Here In My Heart

by
Betsy Harris

Troll Associates

Library of Congress Cataloging-in-Publication Data

Harris, Betsy.
  Here in my heart / by Betsy Harris.
    p.   cm.—(Hampstead High; 2)
  Summary: A shy and self-conscious aspiring poet finds herself
attracted to the leader of a student rock band.
  ISBN 0-8167-1911-X (pbk.)
  [1. Performing arts—Fiction.   2. High schools—Fiction.
3. Schools—Fiction.]   I. Title.   II. Series: Harris, Betsy.
Hampstead High; 2.
PZ7.H2409He   1991
[Fic]—dc20   89-20419

A TROLL BOOK, published by Troll Associates

Copyright © 1992 by Troll Associates

Printed in the United States of America.

10 9 8 7 6 5 4 3 2 1

Here In My Heart

Chapter One

Karen Gillespie sat at her desk in the back row and chewed on the end of her pen cap. In front of the classroom, her English teacher, Ms. Davis, was talking about the poems of Wordsworth; but Karen's mind was elsewhere. She stared down at a page of her notebook at the two lines she had just written:

> My heart's drawn to you
> Like a moth to a flame…

She liked the image, but where should she go with it? What rhyme scheme? "Flame"…"insane" …no, that wasn't a real rhyme anyway. "Game"… "name"…now that was more like it. "I something something something/At the sound of your name…"

Karen pushed her light brown hair back from her eyes. Her hair was straight and shiny, with golden highlights—all of which Karen failed to notice. She wore mostly long, dark skirts and baggy sweaters—clothes that hid her slim figure. Her most attractive feature was her large hazel eyes, but not many people looked at her long enough to realize how appealing they were, or to sense the brightness and warmth behind them. Which suited Karen just fine. She didn't like calling attention to herself.

She took the pen out of her mouth and looked at it with a shudder. It really was a gross habit. She'd *have* to quit doing that. People already thought she was a little strange; she didn't need to give them something else to talk about. She knew that gossipy Penny Ferris had told Jennifer McSwain that she thought Karen was weird and that Karen didn't like people, which wasn't true at all.

It was just that...well, she felt shy and out of place with people sometimes, especially when she was with a *lot* of people. She hated when it happened, but she couldn't help it. She'd get all tongue-tied and then be sure that everyone was staring at her, which only made it worse. She felt like dying when that happened. She figured it was better to stay away from the spotlight; there were always plenty of kids competing for that anyway.

So Karen always sat in the back during classes. But that had its advantages, too. If an idea for a poem or a song lyric came to her, like it had just now, she could easily tune out what was going on around her and get it down on paper. Luckily, she was able to get good grades even though she sometimes missed what was said in class.

Now she bent her head and wrote a couple of new lines and sat back to look at the result:

> My heart's drawn to you
> Like a moth to a flame,

I hear heavenly music
When I hear your name...

It might work as a lyric, with an up-tempo beat, if she could—

"Karen!" Ms. Davis's voice cut sharply into her thoughts. She sounded irritated. She must have called on her a few times before Karen had come back to earth.

"Yes, Ms. Davis?"

"I hate to intrude on your valuable time, Karen, but could you tell us, please, to what was Wordsworth referring in the line, 'Ethereal minstrel! Pilgrim of the sky!'"

Karen quickly closed her notebook to hide her own attempt at poetry and tried to remember the Wordswoth poem that she had read the night before.

"Uh, yes, sorry. He was, um, talking about a skylark."

Ms. Davis nodded, but she still didn't look very happy. After all, this was the third time Karen had been caught in English with her mind elsewhere—and it was only the third week of school! "Could you tell the class the meaning of the word 'ethereal'?"

"It means 'heavenly,' 'from heaven,' something like that."

"Correct. Why does Wordsworth call the skylark an 'ethereal minstrel'?"

Three questions in a row! Ms. Davis was *definitely* not happy with her. She'd answer this one, and then, hopefully, someone else would have to answer questions about this dumb bird.

"Because it makes such sweet music. He is saying that beautiful things, like music and poetry, come from heaven, or at least they're inspired by heaven." She sounded like a machine. *This is a recording.*

"Very good, Karen. Try to stay with us, will you?"

Ms. Davis turned her attention to someone else at last. But Karen felt that everyone's eyes were still on her, everyone was smirking at how much she was blushing. For today, at least, writing time was over. It would have to be Wordsworth until the bell rang at the end of the hour.

The trouble was, she didn't really like Wordsworth much. Or Byron, or a lot of the other stuff they were reading in this eleventh-grade lit class. Maybe if they studied some new poems, or better yet, some great song lyrics—they were poetry too, weren't they? But Wordsworth! She had a feeling that kids would be able to get into English more if all the things they read weren't practically prehistoric. If she had *her* way...

The bell rang, ending English for the day. Piling her books together, Karen headed for the door. But as she neared it, Ms. Davis stopped her. "Karen, may I see you for a moment?"

Uh-oh. With her books clutched to her chest, she stood by Ms. Davis's desk while the rest of the class filed out, waiting for the worst.

Ms. Davis sat down and studied her for a few seconds. "Karen, I've looked at your records. Clearly, you're a bright girl, and most of your teachers have thought very highly of you."

Karen shifted from one foot to the other in silence.

"Which makes it all the more difficult for me to understand why it is that you are having so much trouble paying attention in this class. You don't seem to be able to keep your mind where it's supposed to be. I've had to speak to you about this too often since the term began. And there have been other times—when I *didn't* call on you— when I could tell that you were daydreaming and not focusing on what we were doing."

"I'm sorry. I'll try to do better."

"Is everything all right, Karen? Is there some personal problem? Some trouble at home? Anything that would account for your wandering off the way you do?"

Karen's eyes were fixed on the tile floor. Could she possibly tell Ms. Davis that Wordsworth *bored* her? *No way.* What then? She had to say *something*. "Um, no, it's nothing like that. I just…it…I'll try to pay more attention."

"Well, see that you do. It would be a shame if this habit of yours had a bad effect on your grades." The teacher gave her one last, searching look, then turned to her record book. "That'll be all—for now."

"Thank you, Ms. Davis."

As she headed for her locker to dump her books before going to lunch, Karen felt relieved. At least that was over. It could've been worse, she knew. Why did she float off to a dream world that way? Maybe because she could control it better than the real world.

She headed for the cafeteria, bought a small container of milk and a sandwich, and looked around the room. It was crowded, as always, and noisy. There was shrill laughter, clinking silverware, and the combined sound of two hundred conversations. But over the din she heard a voice calling her name.

"Karen! Over here!"

In the far corner of the big room, her best friend, Gwen Morgan, was waving frantically. Next to her was an empty seat that she had been saving. Karen went over to join her.

Gwen was tall and blond. The girls had been friends for years, spending some time in each other's company almost every day. Until last summer neither of them had dated, or even paid that much attention to boys. Gwen had always been a skinny, straight-haired tomboy with glasses. Now, suddenly, curves had replaced the bony angles of her body, the hated glasses had given way to contact lenses, and boys had become a much more frequent topic in her conversation. One boy in particular took up a lot of her attention. Gwen thought Phil Cassidy was "to die for." Phil had recently broken up with Jeannie Fox, and Gwen hoped that he'd take some notice of her—and find the new Gwen worth pursuing.

"You're late," she said, as Karen slid into the seat she'd saved. "I had to fight to keep this chair for you."

"Sorry. Ms. Davis kept me after class for not paying attention. I better watch it in English."

But Gwen was too full of her own news to sympathize much. "You'll never believe what happened this morning!" she practically shouted. "I've been waiting to tell you. I thought I was going to *die*!"

Karen smiled. Gwen had always been dramatic, and she usually was able to take Karen out of her gloomier moods. "All right, don't keep me in suspense. What happened?"

Gwen shoved her cafeteria tray aside—she hadn't eaten anything on it—leaned in close, and spoke in a low, confidential tone. "Phil Cassidy came up to me after homeroom today. You know, we're in the same social studies class first period. Anyway, he asked if he could walk to class with me! And he asked me if I wanted to go with him to the pep rally and School Spirit Dance this Friday! Can you *believe* it? I thought I would just die right there! It was all I could do to tell him yes! He is so *cute*! Oh, what am I going to *wear*? You've got to come over one day this week and help me decide, okay?"

"Sure," Karen agreed unenthusiastically.

Gwen tilted her head and gave her friend a curious look. "Are you all right? You look kind of down today."

"No, no, I'm fine, really. It's nothing."

"Hey, maybe someone'll ask *you* to go on Friday. Maybe we could double!"

"Me? Oh, no, I don't think so. But that's really great about Phil. He seems like a nice guy."

But Gwen would not be discouraged. She was feeling so happy about her good fortune that she wanted her best friend to share in it. "I bet there's lots of nice guys who still don't have dates for Friday night. You never know, right? In fact, I think Jeff Whitman may have a crush on you." Jeff was an editor on the school newspaper, the *Clarion*.

"Jeff Whitman? Come on, Gwen. You know boys aren't interested in me. I'm not pretty and I'm too quiet. Let's face it, no boy is going to ask me to the dance. And certainly not Jeff Whitman. Besides, he's only interested in the paper."

"That's not true! If you'd just try a little...you know...try to make conversation with some boy in the hall or after school, to show you're interested. And do a *little* something with makeup—not too much, nothing bizarre—just a little blush and eye shadow and..."

Karen shook her head. They'd had this talk before. The fact was that Karen had never considered herself attractive—so why bother with makeup? Okay, maybe she did have a nice smile and kind of nice eyes. But she couldn't believe that Jeff Whitman or any other boy would lose any sleep over her.

"Oh, by the way, I almost forgot," said Gwen, fumbling through her purse. "I brought those poems you gave me to read." She pulled out a sheaf of notebook paper and handed it to Karen. "You know, you're really talented. I mean, these are *good*! Some of them are wonderful, especially that one about the girl who wants to go away from her old hometown and see the world....'Born to Wander,' and the one called 'You Don't Have to Ask.' They'd make great songs. Did you ever think about becoming a songwriter?"

Karen had actually spent a lot of time thinking about being a songwriter and a singer. But those dreams were so far removed from reality, so private, that she'd never shared them, even with Gwen. "How could I be a songwriter? I don't write music, and I'd never be able to sing in front of anyone."

Gwen dismissed her concerns. "What about writing the words and giving them to someone else to write the music? A musical partnership?" Suddenly Gwen's face lit up. "Someone dreamy and talented—like Don Stanton. Now there's an idea. I bet the two of you could make beautiful music together," she finished with a sly grin.

Don Stanton was bass player and lead singer of a group he'd started called the Sevilles. They were a really hot band and played lots of dances. They'd even appeared on local television. Don also wrote some of their songs. All the girls in Hampstead High thought he was gorgeous. Although he didn't have one steady girlfriend, Don was usually surrounded by the most popular females at Hampstead. A crowd of interested girls always gathered when the Sevilles were playing at school dances or other affairs.

Karen didn't know Don personally, but she knew who he was. He was tall and slender, with a mop of light brown hair and bright blue eyes. She'd heard the Sevilles play a few times, and she liked the way he moved with the music. He sang well, with a sexy voice. But she didn't think much of the songs he'd written. Gwen was right; he could use a songwriter. But certainly not her!

Gwen suddenly pointed to the far end of the cafeteria. "There's Don now. Let's just take these over to him and ask him what he thinks. Maybe he'll love 'em, and you and he can become a big-time songwriting team...."

In her growing excitement, Gwen had stood up and was waving to Don with Karen's poems in her

9

hand. She was clearly on the verge of rushing right over to where he was eating lunch with his friends. A couple of kids were staring at them, and Karen felt her face getting all red.

"Gwen!" she snapped. "Don't you *dare* go over there! Will you please sit down and stop making a scene? Everyone's looking at us!"

Gwen dropped her arm and sank back into her chair. Karen grabbed the poems from her and stuck them into a notebook. "I couldn't show these to Don Stanton. He doesn't even know who I am. Besides, they're just not good enough."

"Of course they're good enough," Gwen argued. "And can you think of a better way to get to know Don than using the direct approach?" She continued, grinning at Karen. "Maybe you haven't noticed, but Don Stanton is one hot number. And you have the perfect excuse to go over and meet him. Who knows? Maybe lightning will strike when he meets you—a girl who's pretty *and* writes great song lyrics. And at the very least, he can look over your poems."

Karen couldn't help smiling at her friend's optimism. "Gwen, I know you *mean* well, but… well, I can't just walk up to him and say, 'Here, read this and tell me if we can write hit songs together.' I'd feel like a total idiot."

Gwen sighed and shook her head. "You know, I wish you'd give yourself more credit. You don't think you're pretty, and you are, and you think everybody thinks you're weird, and they don't."

"Well, Penny Ferris and Jennifer McSwain do."

"Oh, please! What do you care what Jennifer McSwain and her friends think anyway? Plus, it'd be easy to make people realize they're wrong about you." Gwen grabbed Karen's shoulders and gently shook her. "You know, you should make some kind of a junior year resolution. Make this the year that people get to know you better. I bet you anything that you'll be a lot happier if you do. You're a special person, Karen. Smart and funny and pretty, even if you don't believe it. Let the world know what I know. That I'm lucky to have you for my best friend."

Karen stared at Gwen and blinked away a couple of tears. "I'm lucky to have *you* as a best friend too. And thanks for what you said." She sighed. "I'll think about it. I really will."

The bell rang, and hundreds of chairs were pushed back as everyone got ready for afternoon classes. Gwen looked down at her untouched food. "How can I be expected to *eat*, knowing I've got a date with Phil Cassidy this week? See you later, after school?"

"Umm, no, I've got a meeting of the editorial staff." Karen's one extracurricular activity was the school paper, the *Clarion*. The only time her poems had ever appeared in print was in the *Clarion*'s creative arts column. And Karen was secretly thrilled when they were published.

Gwen started to dash off, then stopped abruptly, and turned back to Karen. "And will you think about showing some of your work to Don? What have you got to lose?"

Karen smiled, and replied, "I'll think about it. Really." But what Gwen didn't understand was that Karen had a *lot* to lose. The poems were everything to Karen. And she couldn't deal with opening herself up to someone like Don Stanton. What if he didn't like them—or her?

Chapter Two

When Karen walked into the *Clarion* office, there were already little knots of people scattered around the room deep in discussions.

"Karen! Hi!" Jeff Whitman spotted her and broke away from his little group to greet her. He was the Features Editor of the *Clarion*, responsible for the creative arts column. He was an intense-looking guy, about five-ten with jet-black hair and piercing eyes under heavy brows. He dressed in preppy, conservative clothes, like the chinos, blue-and-white-striped shirt, and V-necked pullover he was wearing now. He was very attractive—in an intellectual sort of way. He gave Karen his serious smile as she approached.

He was all business. "Listen, Karen, it'd be great if you have any poems for the next issue; we're kind of light on good stuff."

Karen thought a moment, then leafed through her notebook. "How about this one?" she asked, handing him a sheet of paper.

Jeff read it through quickly, then read the first stanza out loud:

"The Difference

What's the difference
What clothes I choose to wear,
How I want to keep my hair,
If my bedroom isn't neat,
Whether I watch what I eat,
The world just goes its own way,
Makes no difference what I do or say..."

He looked up and gave Karen a warmer smile. "This is intense. It may be a little strong for Mr. Wadleigh, but let's go with it." Mr. Wadleigh was the *Clarion* faculty advisor. "You can really create a mood, Karen. I mean, I understand how the person in that poem feels."

"Glad you like it," Karen said shyly.

"Not just *like* it, I think it's fabulous! You're really talented. I'd love to see more of your writing —maybe we could, uh, get together and talk about it sometime if you like." Jeff gave her an intense look.

"Sure, sometime." Karen was surprised at the offer. Could Gwen possibly be right about his being interested in her? If so, it might be a good time to start putting Gwen's ideas about being friendlier to people into practice.

"Sure, if you want. I could show you some other stuff."

Jeff nodded. "Great! Great! Hey, I tell you what, after this meeting is over, if you like we could—"

"Jeff Whitman?" Jeff broke off and looked over Karen's shoulder at the person who'd asked for him. Karen turned to see none other than Don

Stanton standing there in the doorway with a large envelope in his hand. He waved the package. "Got those publicity shots you wanted. Pick what you like best." His eyes shifted to Karen and he said, "Hi."

"Hi," she answered.

Jeff looked from her to Don, and seemed at a loss for a second before he could speak. "Oh yeah, right, sure, Don. Let's take a look. Oh, you know Karen Gillespie, don't you?"

Don gave her a casual smile. "Nice to meet you. How you doin'?"

What a nice smile, she thought to herself. "Hello," she said aloud.

Don dismissed her from his attention and walked over to Jeff's desk to spread out his photographs. Karen noticed that the volume of conversation in the room had dropped off sharply, and that some of the girls on the staff were just gaping at him. But Don didn't seem to notice.

Don and Jeff were bent over the desk, going over the pictures while Karen stood to one side, watching them.

"This is the best one of me," Don said, pointing to one picture. "But the other guys in the band say that they're all in shadow, so they'd prefer *this* one." He picked up another photo, in which all the band members were featured. "And this one, over here, was taken while we were playing at a beach party last summer. I think it's pretty cool, but it's a little blurry. What do you think?"

Jeff picked up one photo after another, gave each one a careful study, and then put it down again. "Each one has its merits," he finally said, "but which conveys the band best..." He concentrated on the photos again.

Don looked up from the pictures. His eyes met Karen's—she was standing there trying to decide if she should wait for Jeff to finish or just walk away. She was feeling silly standing there, unnoticed.

"Karen, what do you think?" Don asked. "Come over here and take a look."

Karen looked uncertain for a moment, then went around the desk and stood between the two boys. She felt a bit lightheaded and couldn't focus on the photos at first. Then she took a deep breath and looked down at the pictures.

"So, what do you think?" Don asked again.

"Well," said Karen, still looking at the photos before her, "if you want my honest opinion, I think you should use the one that features all the members of the band equally."

Don gave her a startled look. "Hey! Wait a minute here. Don't I get any respect for being the *leader?*"

"Sure you do. But still, the group is called the Sevilles, and that's what this picture reflects best." Karen surprised herself with her boldness.

Don took a step back and then gave Karen a more thoughtful look from under quizzical eyebrows. For a moment he almost looked hurt. Then he gave her a broad wink. "Score one for the young lady. She's got a point there. The Sevilles it is. Okay, we'll use this one."

"What's the picture for?" asked Karen.

"The Student Council has just hired the Sevilles to play for the Homecoming Dance next month, and the *Clarion* is going to spread the good news with a feature article along with this *fantastic*

15

photo, which you, Karen...uh...umm..."

"Gillespie," she supplied, with a giggle that embarrassed her even as it came out of her mouth.

"...which *you*, Karen Gillespie, have chosen to show us at our best." He sounded exactly like a TV game show host. As quickly as he had put on the phony dialect, he went back to being Don Stanton. "Seriously, it's the right shot to use. You're absolutely right. Thanks a lot."

"Glad to be of help." Karen assumed their discussion was over, but Don showed no sign of leaving. Jeff, however, showed every sign of being annoyed at all the attention Don was giving her. *What would Gwen do in a situation like this?* Karen wondered.

"So tell me, do you like the Sevilles?" Don asked. "I mean, you've heard us, haven't you?"

"Sure I have."

"Ah, another fan? So what do you think?" He smiled at her.

"I really like the Sevilles," she began. "You've got a great sound and play a good mix of oldies and new stuff. And I like your singing. You've got a great voice."

"Thanks." Don smiled at her again. "You know, some of that 'new stuff' is stuff I write."

Uh-oh. Karen had hoped the subject would not come up. She was a terrible liar, and she did not want to tell Don what she thought of his song lyrics. He seemed like a nice guy, and she didn't want to hurt his feelings. "I know," she said. "You've written some great tunes."

Don gave her a searching look, then said, "Somehow, I sense a 'but' coming." He cocked his head, as if to look at her from a different angle. "You know how often a girl tells me something she thinks I don't want to hear? Never, that's how often."

Karen picked up one of the photographs and kept her eyes on it. "Why?"

"Because they're Fans," he said. "With a capital F. If you have something to say, I'd like to hear it."

"Karen's a writer herself," put in Jeff.

"Well, all right, then! I knew we had something in common. So tell me—as one writer to another— what you think of my songs."

Karen put down the picture, but wouldn't look up at him. "Well, the music's great. It really is. But the words are sort of the same old thing. 'Party, party, party,' or 'Baby, baby, baby,' or 'You're a neat chick and I'm a cool dude, so let's get together.' You know what I mean? It's sort of, I don't know, boring."

"Then it'd be more interesting if I wrote things like, 'Gonna study French irregular verbs tonight,' or 'You're kind of dull and I'm real bored, guess I'll go home and read a book.'"

"Well, not that, but…"

"Or, 'Oh, boy, it's study-hall time!'"

"No!" Karen was getting annoyed. He had asked her for her opinion, and now he was making fun of her. "There're only so many things to write songs about, so the trick is to find new ways of saying the same old things, that's all."

"And I don't?"

"Well… I haven't heard everything you've written, but no, not that I've heard."

He nodded slowly. "Well. Thank you so much

for enlightening me."

Karen could feel a blush coming on. Not only had she hurt his feelings, but she was making a fool of herself. "I'm sorry, but...you asked me what I thought, so I told you."

"Right, so I did. Well, it seemed like a good idea at the time." He turned abruptly to Jeff. "Anyway, does that take care of our business? We've picked out the picture to go with the story, and if you need any information, you know how to get in touch. Is that all?"

Jeff made a show of being caught up with his papers, then looked up. "Huh? Oh, right, yeah. That's all I need. Thanks, Don. We'll give you a nice spread next issue."

"Fantastic," Don said sarcastically as he waved a casual goodbye. His eyes caught Karen's, and he made a little bow and tipped an imaginary hat. "I surely do thank you for your opinion." And he was gone.

As the door swung shut behind him, Karen stood looking at it, chewing her lower lip. Then she faced Jeff. "I shouldn't have said all that. I don't know what came over me—criticizing his songs. And now I've hurt his feelings."

Jeff was supportive. "He asked what you thought, and you told him. You did exactly what you should have."

"Oh, I know he asked me. But I should've stuck to a nice, simple white lie. It wouldn't have been such a big deal. I wish—"

"Karen, you're making too much of it. He'll recover. I mean, he's probably forgotten it already. After all, he's just a rock singer. It's not like you just insulted Shakespeare or something. As far as I'm concerned, one of your poems is better than all the rock songs I've ever heard."

Karen looked at Jeff. He was serious! He certainly wanted to make her feel better. Karen smiled at the revelation.

"I mean it," Jeff insisted. "See, you're an *artist*, and he's just an entertainer. His audience is all the kids who don't want anything more than good parties on weekends, but you write for people who want to *think*."

She shook her head. "It's not that, exactly. I don't know about everyone else, but I know I like to think, and I also like a lot of rock songs. Sometimes if you listen to the words of a song, it makes your brain work. But if you just listen to the music and feel the beat, it makes you *feel* better. There are some great rock songs."

"Sure there are," Jeff agreed immediately. "But it's like cotton candy—it tastes good for a second, and then it's gone. Sometimes the words are clever, but there's no *real* brain food there. Well, *you* know what I mean."

Actually, Karen didn't. For her, rock was a lot more meaningful. But before she had a chance to reply, their conversation was interrupted.

"Hey, Jeff!" A stocky kid with a plastic pocket protector full of pens was holding up a sheet of paper. "You gotta okay this layout before I leave!"

"Okay, Brian, be right over." Jeff turned back to Karen and spoke quietly. "Listen, if you don't have other plans…do you feel like going to that dance Friday night? I mean, with me?"

Karen hoped she didn't look as shocked as she

felt. Gwen was right about Jeff. Only she hadn't seen it coming and didn't know what to say. Jeff Whitman was asking her out on a date! He was serious and nice and cute. Maybe she was coming out of her shell at last. Wait till she told Gwen! Suddenly she realized that she had been standing there silently a little too long.

"I'm sorry. It's just that I'm a little surprised."

"Don't be." He glanced over at the impatient Brian. "I think we'll have a good time. We'll have a chance to *really* talk—without all these interruptions. So, you want to go?"

At that point, Karen managed an answer. "Yes, thanks, that'd be very nice. I'd love to."

"Great! Look, I'll talk to you later in the week about the details, okay?"

"Fine."

"Hey, Jeff!" Brian was glaring across the room at him. "Sometime today, all right?"

"Coming." He gave Karen a serious smile. "Well...see you later."

"See you," replied Karen, as she walked out into the hall. Her first real date with a boy! Jeff was a great guy—she should be thrilled!

So how come she was thinking about Don Stanton?

Chapter Three

"Mom! What time is it?" Karen peered at her reflection in the bathroom mirror, and wondered if she had time to wash her face and start over. She wasn't used to wearing makeup, and the face in the mirror was a stranger's. She studied her eyebrows and picked up the eyebrow pencil. Was the left brow thicker than the right? They certainly weren't even. That eye shadow, recommended by Gwen, was *much* too much. The blusher was not subtle enough, and as for the hair...well, the hair was what it was and she'd have to live with it.

Her mother's voice came faintly through the door. "Hurry up, dear! It's seven-fifteen! Your date will be here in a few minutes!"

It was *her* first date, and her parents were acting like this was the most important event in *their* lives. Well, she couldn't get too angry with them, knowing they meant well. She loved them, but if her father should pop up with his camera and try to get a snapshot of the couple before they left the house, she was simply going to crawl under the living-room rug and stay there until everyone went away and she could die in peace.

On the other hand, her eleven-year-old brother, Joey, had been treating the Big Date as a Big Yawn. While Mom and Dad were impressed by Jeff's position on the school paper and his being among the top students in their class in terms of grades, none of that made any difference to Joey.

All he wanted to know was, "Does he play football? Can he play guitar?" When the answers to these questions turned out to be no, Joey knew all he had to about Jeff Whitman. He was a geek.

Now he was banging on the bathroom door. "Are you gonna be in there *all night*? *Other* people sometimes want to get in there too, you know."

Karen stuffed the scattered makeup back into her purse. "I'll be out in a minute. Why don't you use the downstairs bathroom, anyway?"

"Because I left my new comic book in *this* bathroom. Come on, already. You could spend a week in there and you'd still come out looking the same!"

For a moment Karen considered ripping up her brother's precious comic book, or even just tearing out the last page. But that was utterly juvenile behavior. Instead, she turned to give herself one last look in the full-length mirror on the door.

With Gwen's help, she had chosen her outfit with care. It was a different look for her, but she kind of liked it. The turquoise sweater Gwen had convinced her to buy really brought out the blue in her eyes. And her friend's black jeans fit her snugly, showing off her slim waist. As she raised a hand to her hair, she heard the ring of the front-door chimes. *Oh well*, she thought. *Too late to do anything about it now*.

"Honey! Jeff is here," called her father from the foot of the stairs.

"Be right down," she called back, opening the door. She took a deep breath, and descended the stairs.

Jeff, wearing a tweed jacket over an open-collared, button-down blue shirt, sat in the least comfortable chair in the living room. Her parents sat together on the couch, grinning at him brightly. Joey stood off to one side, arms crossed, looking both bored and scornful.

As she reached the bottom of the stairs, she heard her mother say, "Karen tells me that you work on the school paper, Jeff. That sounds very exciting. Are you thinking of a career in journalism?"

"When I was your age," Mr. Gillespie piped in, "I thought I might be a musician, but I outgrew *that* pretty quick."

Jeff spoke first to Mrs. Gillespie. "As a matter of fact, I am considering a career in journalism. I'm planning on working on the newspaper in college as well."

"Are you thinking of going away to college, or staying in this area?" asked Mr. Gillespie.

"I'm in the process of evaluating a number of schools," Jeff replied. "I haven't yet made up my mind."

"Hi, Jeff!" said Karen brightly. He stood quickly and smiled at her.

"Well, you look wonderful, dear," said Mrs. Gillespie. "Jeff, it was a pleasure to meet you. Now you two have a lovely time at that dance."

"Thanks, Mom."

"Drive carefully, Jeff," added Mr. Gillespie.

"And be sure that you're home by twelve."

"All *right*, Daddy. Bye!"

"Nice to meet you, Mrs. Gillespie, Mr. Gillespie," called Jeff as he followed Karen out the front door.

"Sorry about all the questions," Karen said as they got in the car.

Jeff looked straight ahead as he began driving. "That's okay," he said. "I enjoyed it. Your folks are interesting."

Karen gave him a sidelong glance. *He's serious,* she realized. Jeff probably found parents more interesting than their kids. He was a serious guy.

"But they *can* be too much, sometimes," she said.

Jeff shrugged as they pulled into the school parking lot.

Unlike the big dances such as the prom, which were held in the gym, the School Spirit Dance was held in the cafeteria. The tables had been folded and stored; the chairs were lined up against the walls. Red and white streamers were hung from walls and ceiling, and a huge banner was strung across the width of the room that read GO VIKINGS! On the raised stage, the deejay was fussing with his turntables, one on either side of his chair. He was a short, wiry guy in a loud, flowery Hawaiian shirt and mirrored sunglasses. Finishing with the turntables, he leaned forward to his mike.

"Testing, one, two, three, testing. This is a test. One, two, three. Hear me all right, back there?"

"We hear you!" yelled a kid who stood with a small group of early arrivals at the far end of the room.

"Dynamite. We're just about ready to party. Stand by, folks."

Along one wall was a refreshment table with bowls of punch and platters of munchies. Karen and Jeff headed for the table to say hello to Mr. Wadleigh, the *Clarion* advisor. As they chatted, Gwen and Phil joined them. Then Mr. Wadleigh wandered off to keep an eye on the halls and parking lot.

"How was the pep rally?" asked Karen.

Gwen rolled her eyes and Phil grinned. They were wearing matching red and white sweat shirts with VIKINGS across the front. "Well," said Gwen, "the cheerleaders were *very* peppy, but the band needs work, and two twirlers dropped their batons. Hi, Jeff."

"Hi."

"Coach Bliss made the same speech from last year," added Phil.

"Oh, I bet he's used that speech for twenty years," Gwen said. "Too much trouble to learn a new one. As pep rallies go, it was about average."

"And the team needs a couple of good running backs," put in Phil.

"*I* have a great idea!" Gwen exclaimed. "Let's make a trade with Lincoln High. Give them Coach Bliss and Jennifer McSwain for two running backs and two twirlers!"

"We could throw in the lunchroom cook, too," suggested Phil.

"That'll kill the trade," said Karen. "Anyway, I think Coach Bliss looks cute in his baseball cap."

"Great outfit, Karen!" Gwen had seen Karen try it on at least half a dozen times.

"Thanks," replied Karen with a straight face. "And I love your sweat shirts."

"Got 'em at the school store," said Phil.

"It's his first gift to me," said Gwen, holding out her arms and spinning around to show it off. "I'm going to have it framed." They grinned at each other. Karen was happy to see that they were getting along so well.

Jeff had gotten very quiet, so Gwen turned to him. "So, Jeff, how are you doing?"

"Oh, fine, thanks." He looked a little bored.

Maybe he's not into small talk, Karen thought as she jumped into the awkward silence. "Jeff's got some great stuff in the next *Clarion*. Wait'll you see it."

"Ever write any sports stuff?" asked Phil.

"No. I'm the Features Editor."

"What's 'Features'?"

"Like a big story about Don Stanton and the Sevilles," Karen jumped in. "They're going to play at the Homecoming Dance."

Phil brightened. "The Sevilles are playing for homecoming? No kiddin'! That's great, those guys are really hot!"

Their conversation was interrupted by the shout of the deejay. "*All ri-i-i-i-ight,* all you Vikings, this is your man Rockmaster Robbie, and I'm gonna spin the hottest, the heaviest, the funkiest sounds around. Get ready, grab your date, don't hesitate, bop till you drop, 'cause...IT'S PARTY TIME! Let's rock!"

A heavy riff on drums and guitar signaled the start of the dance, and couples were already out on the floor. Phil grabbed Gwen's hand. "Let's go!"

As he pulled her out to dance, Gwen turned back and yelled, "Have fun, you two! Catch you later!"

Karen watched Gwen's blonde hair fly as her friend began to move to the music. She turned to Jeff. Was he going to ask her to dance? It didn't look like it. Jeff was frowning at the dance floor.

"Let's find a place to sit where the music isn't deafening and we can talk," he said to Karen.

They went down to the far end of the cafeteria.

"That's a little better," Jeff said as they sat. "You can't hear yourself think over there...I don't know why they have to play it so loud."

"It's *supposed* to be loud. Most of the kids aren't here to talk." Karen looked longingly at the dance floor. Alone in her room, she often danced to music. Somehow, it helped her forget all her problems. But here, surrounded by so many people, she felt too self-conscious.

"Personally," said Jeff, "I'd rather have a conversation, exchange ideas, and discuss issues, than jump around like a maniac."

"Oh, I like to talk, too," she said, looking out at the swirling activity of the other kids. "But don't you ever wish you could just get up and shut off your brain and...*move* like that, without thinking about it, without thinking about anything?"

"Shut off your brain?" Jeff stared at her. "No, I don't follow you. I mean, I could understand most of these other kids saying that—they almost never turn their brains *on*. But *you*—you're different from most of them. You actually *can* think. Why would you want *not* to?"

Karen shrugged. "I don't know."

"You see?" Jeff sounded triumphant. "It's that music. Mindless words. Listen to enough of it and your mind goes blank."

"Not all the words are mindless. Some rock lyrics are very good poetry."

"Well, maybe." Jeff didn't sound convinced. "But how can you understand them when the music is deafening?"

"Well, when you want to follow the words, you don't turn it up so loud. But tonight really isn't for listening and thinking."

Jeff shook his head. "What a goal! Jump around until you're completely exhausted. Some fun."

"Don't you like to have fun?" Karen asked.

"Well, sure I do. Like going to a movie or a play, maybe playing a game of chess." He smiled down at Karen. "Or talking to an intelligent girl."

Karen flushed with pleasure at the compliment. "Jeff, can I ask you something?" she said.

"Sure."

"Why did you want to come here tonight?"

He leaned back and folded his arms across his chest. "I haven't come to these things much before. But I think it's a good idea to go and check them out from now on. See, I've got plans for the future. Next year I want to be Editor-in-Chief of the *Clarion*, and I was even thinking about running for Student Council. To be successful, it's important to be able to relate to other students. So I came to observe, you might say. And I figured you'd be interested, too."

"In observing?"

"You're a writer, aren't you? Don't writers need to get ideas and material from someplace?"

Karen nodded. For the first time, she got a clear picture of her life. Jeff was right: Karen had always been just an observer. Maybe now was the time to start getting involved in the world a little more...

Jeff shifted uncomfortably in his seat at her silence. "Anyway, I'd feel real stupid getting out on the dance floor," he said lamely.

He's just as shy as I am, Karen realized. *But he won't admit it.* Perhaps everyone felt a little nervous inside.

"Well, what do you know—it's the members of the press!" Don Stanton stood grinning down at them. With him was Jennifer McSwain. She was a tall brunette, flawlessly made-up and dressed. She might have stepped right out of an ad in some magazine.

"You two having fun?" asked Don.

"Uh-huh," replied Karen. "How are you, Don? Hi, Jennifer."

Jennifer smiled in a cool fashion, but she didn't say anything. Her eyes roamed the cafeteria, obviously finding lots of places where she would rather be than standing there. But Don didn't seem to notice. He continued to stand, hands in the pockets of his faded jeans, looking at Karen and Jeff.

"I'm surprised to find *you* here, Karen."

"Why?"

"Oh, I just didn't think the quality of the music tonight would be up to your standards." He winked broadly at Jennifer, who giggled and gave him a worshipful look.

Karen was relieved that the lights were low enough so that her blush wouldn't show. "My standards aren't all that high. I like a lot of these songs, actually." Her eyes wanted to wander off, but she forced herself to look straight at Don.

Don turned to Jennifer. "Did you know that Karen here is a real, genuine music critic? She must be here to review the choice of records tonight, for *Rolling Stone* or something."

Jeff said, "Now wait a minute…"

"It's all right," said Karen. She stood up and faced Don. "I'm not a critic. I never said I was. All I did was answer a question you asked. I said I liked your band, and your singing, but that I didn't love your lyrics. That's all."

"What does *she* know, anyway," huffed Jennifer. "Oh, there's Penny and Tina and Chuck over there! Come on, Donny, let's go; what are we wasting time with *these* two for?" She tugged at his arm impatiently.

"All I did was to be honest," Karen went on. "You said you wanted a straight answer, and I gave you one. Next time, I'll know better. You just want to be flattered."

Don seemed to want to say something else, but Jennifer insisted, "*Donn-eee! Come on!*" He let himself be pulled away, looking back at Karen once before he melted into the crowd.

Karen sank back down next to Jeff, who asked, "Are you all right? He was being a real creep."

She took a deep breath and let it out, feeling more in control of herself. "Oh, it's no big deal. He's not used to anyone telling him something he doesn't want to hear, that's all. I'm surprised he was still thinking about it four days later."

At that moment Gwen flopped down onto the chair next to Karen. She was gasping, and her hair was plastered in ringlets to her forehead.

"Hi, there! Phil's getting some punch. Phil's an absolutely fabulous dancer! I feel like I just ran a marathon! Say, was that Don Stanton I saw walking away just now? With Her Royal Highness Princess Jennifer?"

"That's who it was, all right."

Gwen whispered into Karen's ear, "So, did you ask him about looking your poems over?"

"Of course not!"

"Well, why not? This is the perfect opportunity."

"Gwen, trust me. This was definitely *not* the time to ask him. There may never be a time."

"Why, what—"

"Never mind. I'll tell you later. Full report tomorrow, okay?"

Phil approached carrying two cups of punch, his sweat shirt sleeves rolled up and his face shining with sweat. "Here you go, Gwen. Drink your punch and let's go!"

Gwen gave a dramatic sigh. "Listen, Karen, if my poor heart gives out in the middle of a number, you can have my beige sweater, the one you're crazy about. I don't know how long I can keep this up. The man is a dancing maniac!" She drained her cup in a single gulp and jumped to her feet. Quickly, she bent over and whispered to Karen, "Isn't he an absolute *doll*? See you guys. Bye, Jeff."

The voice of Rockmaster Robbie came over the sound system: "Now, let's change the mood a little. Here's a dreamy ballad so you can cuddle up and get romantic for a bit." Karen looked over to Jeff, and decided to be a little brave.

"How about trying a slow dance? You want to?"

31

Jeff's attitude toward rock evidently didn't apply to ballads. "Uh, sure," he answered, getting up and leading her out onto the floor.

At first he held her very carefully, as if she were a delicate and fragile piece of glassware that might easily break. Their movements were stiff and awkward. But then they slowly relaxed and their dancing grew more natural. They drifted across the dance floor. *So this is what it's like to be part of a couple,* Karen thought. Yet, something seemed to be missing.

Then she saw Don and Jennifer dance by, and her heart gave a funny flip. Don looked at her, and for a moment, their eyes locked. Then Jennifer said something to him, and he turned his attention back to her.

"Say, Karen?" Jeff returned her to reality.

"Yes?"

"Would you like to do something next weekend —maybe a movie or something?"

Karen felt unsure. She liked Jeff well enough, although he *was* a bit too serious. Yet the way Don Stanton had looked at her before had sent butterflies to her stomach. But Don Stanton wasn't interested in her, she reminded herself. He had Jennifer McSwain. And Jeff really was a sweet person.

"Sure," she said aloud. "A movie sounds fine."

"Great!" said Jeff, smiling at her.

This dating stuff was getting pretty complicated, Karen realized. Life was certainly easier when she had stayed in her little cocoon.

Chapter Four

Karen spent Monday avoiding Jeff Whitman. She just didn't know how she felt about him. At lunch, she had hoped to talk to Gwen about it, but she was sitting with Phil Cassidy. They had invited her to join them, but they'd been so completely involved in each other that she had felt like a fifth wheel.

Karen had mixed feelings about this romance between Gwen and Phil. On one hand, she was happy for Gwen, who was, after all, her best friend. But on the other hand, she was afraid Gwen wouldn't be as available to her, now that she had Phil in her life. The thought of not having Gwen around was depressing. Besides, she didn't have a lot of friends to begin with.

So she spent Monday feeling a bit sorry for herself.

On Tuesday the new issue of the *Clarion* arrived. During homeroom she had quickly checked to make sure that they had printed her poem without any mistakes, and there, smiling up at her from the opposite page, was Don Stanton and his band. She had to admit that he photographed well.

She was walking from her French class to

chemistry later that morning when she heard her name being called behind her. She turned to look, and there was Jeff threading his way through the crowded corridor to catch up.

"Hi!" he said with a big smile. She hoped her smile didn't look as phony as it felt. "Two or three people went out of their way to tell me how much they liked your poem."

"Oh. Great."

"Yeah. So listen, if you have any more, just pass them along, okay?"

"Sure. Well, I better run, I have chemistry all the way over on the other side of the building."

"Well, all right. Oh, Karen?"

"Yes?"

"I was hoping we'd have a chance to talk later about the weekend. Could you meet me in the *Clarion* office after school?"

"Oh...sorry, but I promised my mom I'd be home right after school to help her with some errands."

His face fell. "Too bad. Well...maybe I'll call you later at home, if that's okay."

"All right. Bye."

As she hurried off to chemistry, Karen felt angry at herself. Why had she bothered to tell Jeff a dumb lie like that? Now she *would* have to go right home after classes, or risk the embarrassment of running into him somewhere. And for what?

Obviously, she wasn't sure that she wanted to go out this weekend with Jeff. Why? He was a nice person, smart, and seemed to care for her. Yet he didn't seem to allow himself any fun. And, for the first time in her life, Karen felt ready to jump into life and have some fun—and be with someone fun. Like Don Stanton, for instance.

Now why had *he* popped into her head? A guy like Don would never be interested in a girl like her, so she should just forget about that. Jeff Whitman was more her type. Wasn't he?

Karen felt so confused. Maybe she'd have the chance to talk it all out over lunch with Gwen. But Gwen might be too busy with Phil to have time to talk about her problems. Karen forced all the confusing clutter of questions and doubts to the back of her mind and headed for the chemistry lab. Chemistry presented her with enough problems, without allowing her emotions to confuse her still more.

Karen managed to get through chemistry and English without losing too much concentration, which was something anyway. In lit class, they were reading poems by Emily Dickinson, and she had found her use of imagery breathtaking— especially after Wordsworth. But she was happy to take a lunch break.

As she carried her tray into the cafeteria, her mind returned to her main problem at hand— Jeff Whitman. She was so lost in her thoughts that she didn't hear Gwen call to her at first. She crossed over to where her friend was saving her a seat, and sat next to her. Phil was nowhere in sight.

"For a second I thought you were deliberately ignoring me," Gwen said. She was wearing her red and white VIKINGS sweat shirt again and more makeup than she usually did. "How do you think I'd look with a body wave?"

Karen studied her friend for a moment. Karen

was startled by what she saw. Gwen looked beautiful! Her hair was shiny and pulled back in a flattering French braid. Her eyes were bright with happiness. *Is that what being in love does?* Karen wondered. "You look fantastic." She smiled. "Why would you want to change?"

"Well, Phil was saying that he likes Wendy Swenson's hair, and she has one."

"Well, forget it. You look great, as is. Where is Phil anyway?"

"Oh, he's skipping lunch today. He and Bobby Kramer went to get a tire for Bobby's car. Bobby's dad said he can't use the car with the old tires because it isn't safe, and Bobby and Christine are doubling with Phil and me this Saturday night." Gwen gave her friend a probing look. "Is something the matter? You look like a girl with a problem. What's up?" she asked.

Karen sighed. "I don't know what the problem is, exactly. Jeff wants to go out with me again—"

"Great! It *is* great, isn't it? Or..."

"Well, I just don't know. He's nice and all, but I don't feel anything like what you feel about Phil. I don't really feel like going, but it's not like I've had a lot of offers either. But then again, I don't think it's worth going out with a guy just for the sake of going out with somebody."

Gwen nodded. "Well, I have to admit, you have a point there." She brightened. "But you might enjoy yourself more with him doing something where it's just the two of you. A movie, something like that."

"That's what I was thinking. But I just don't know. I mean, sure he was uncomfortable Friday night. So was I. But we spent a lot of time just talking, and I'm pretty sure he likes me more than I like him."

"And that's bad?"

"Well, it's flattering, I'll admit. But it's awkward, too. Imagine if some boy you didn't care about kept asking you out. Or what if Phil wasn't as interested in you as you were in him? It's not a great situation."

"I suppose. But if I was in *your* shoes—"

"I know, your feet would be killing you—"

"No-o-o-o-o, smart aleck, I was just about to give you some great advice."

"Oh, good! Wait, let me get out a notebook and a pen!"

Gwen rolled her eyes. "Honestly, Karen, I don't know what you've done to deserve a friend like me. Here I am, ready to sympathize and comfort, and you sit there and make bad jokes."

"Sorry! Sorry! I don't know what got into me." Karen grabbed Gwen's arm. "Please give me your wisdom and I'll be grateful to you forever. What should I do, Gwen?"

"Well, I think you should go out with him one more time. Then if you still feel the same way, forget it. But one date's not enough to judge a person—and the guy is crazy about you. Enjoy it a little," Gwen encouraged.

"Well, maybe you're right."

"Of course I am," Gwen stated. "So what are your plans for the weekend, aside from seeing Jeff?"

"Nothing special. Why?"

"I just thought we could get together Friday night and rent a couple of movies and eat three

37

bushels of popcorn and talk about whether or not I should get a body wave. Sound okay?"

"Friday? But I thought you and Phil would be…"

"No, no, we're going out Saturday night. And you'll probably see Jeff Saturday night too. So Friday night we can spend together." Gwen smiled at Karen. "You know, Phil and I may be going together—at least, I *think* we are—but it doesn't mean that I'll be spending all my time with him. I still need to spend time with *you*. And don't you forget it!"

Karen felt her spirits rise. "Friday night, then. It sounds great. And thanks for the advice too."

"Any time. Our help-line is open twenty-four hours a day." Gwen looked at her watch and jumped to her feet. "And now I'd better run off to trig, because if I don't learn all about those equations and formulas and stuff, I may flunk it. And then I'm sure to be grounded until I'm a little old lady. Bye!"

And she was off, carrying her trayful of almost untouched food. Watching her friend go, Karen felt much better. She still wasn't clear on what to do about Jeff, but it didn't appear so serious anymore.

As she went off to history, she passed a loud table full of joking, wisecracking boys. In the midst of them sat Don Stanton. Just then he looked up and caught her eye. Karen bit her lip and kept on walking. She didn't acknowledge him in any way, but her heart was pounding. Out of the corner of her eye, she thought she saw him stand up. She wasn't certain, but it sounded like her name was called out. But in the noisy cafeteria it was impossible to be sure, and she wasn't about to hang around to find out.

After school, Karen started home. It was about a fifteen-minute walk, and when the weather was nice, she enjoyed it. Today was a crisp, cool autumn afternoon, and Karen was taking her time when a car pulled to the curb just in front of her. The driver's door opened, and Don Stanton unfolded his lanky body and stood facing her across the car's roof.

"Hi, Karen."

She nodded. *What does he want?* she wondered.

"Listen, can I say something?"

"What?"

"Well, about the other night. At the dance? I just wanted to say... I was a real jerk. I've felt bad about it ever since. I don't know why I acted like that, but I'm sorry."

"That's all right."

Karen shifted her books from one arm to the other, nervously.

"Say, can I give you a lift anyplace?"

"No, that's okay. I like the walk. Well, I'll be seeing you." Karen wanted to run away, she felt so nervous. Don Stanton had the most intense eyes.

"All right." But Don made no move to get back in his car. He just stood there leaning on the top and looking at her. There was a long silence.

"Well—" Karen started, but Don cut her off.

"Oh yeah, there was one other thing," he said, ducking down to reach something inside the car. He pulled out a copy of the *Clarion* and held it up. "This poem you wrote. I think it's very good."

"Thanks." She wondered if he really liked it, or was only trying to make up for the other night.

"No, really, I like what you do with words. Didn't you have other poems printed in the paper last year?"

"Yes, a few."

"Yeah, I thought so. You're a really good writer, and I wanted to tell you."

"Well…thanks." *This conversation is going around and around,* she thought.

"Actually, I'm not usually as much of a creep as I was at the dance—I must have been in a weird mood or something."

"It's all right."

"Listen, are you *sure* I can't drop you off someplace? It'd be no trouble."

"Oh no, that's okay."

"Positive? I'm a good driver." He gave his car a couple of pats as if to reassure it and Karen at the same time.

Karen smiled and shook her head.

"Tell you what. If you let me drop you off wherever you're going, I'll know you've accepted my apology. Where to? Home? The library? Mexico? You name it."

Karen couldn't help laughing. Don looked so comically desperate. "Your apology is accepted, and you can drop me off at home."

"Fantastic!" He scrambled around and opened the passenger-side door with a deep bow. "Delighted to have you aboard." He slammed her door and ran around to slide into the driver's seat. "Now, if you would tell me where you live…"

Karen gave him the directions. Don's car was

about ten years old, but it was well cared for. It had an expensive-looking cassette deck and a pair of big speakers mounted in the back.

"Nice stereo," commented Karen.

"It ought to be—it took eight weekends of playing at dances and wedding receptions and parties to pay for it."

There was a boxful of cassettes lying by her feet. She picked it up and looked at the titles. Some of them were rock, but there were also a few jazz tapes, and one Beethoven and a Bach.

"You like classical music?"

"I like music, period." They stopped at a red light, and he turned to face her with a solemn expression. "But don't ever tell anyone that I listen to Beethoven. It would ruin my reputation as a cool dude with some kids."

"Your secret is safe with me."

Before she knew it, they had pulled up in front of Karen's house. Once again, Don raced around to open her door with another deep, elaborate bow.

"Can I carry your books to the door? Can I carry *you* to your door?"

Karen stood up and gave him a wry look.

"Okay. I'll just walk you to the door, how's that?"

"That'd be nice."

At the door, she said, "Well, thanks for the lift, Don. See you at school."

"Uh, Karen? About that poem in the paper?"

"Yes?"

"Well, it's written in verses, and each verse ends with the same lines: 'The world just goes its own way/Makes no difference what I do or say.'"

"Right."

"Okay. Now, don't take this the wrong way, because I mean it as a compliment, but I think it'd make a good song lyric."

"You really think so?" Karen felt a rush of excitement. This was a dream come true.

"Absolutely. Tell you what, if you don't mind, I'd like to mess around with it a little, just to see what comes out. All right?"

All right? thought Karen dizzily. *How about wonderful, unbelievable, incredible?* "Sure, if you want to." She even impressed herself with her calmness.

"Great! And listen, when I come up with something, some music for it, I'll give you a call and run it by you. Okay?"

"Sure. I'd love to hear it."

Don whipped out a ballpoint pen and a scrap of paper.

"In that case—and purely for professional reasons, you understand—may I have your phone number?"

Karen gave it to him, feeling dazed by the turn events had taken. He tucked the scrap of paper carefully away in his wallet. *This couldn't really be happening to me, could it?*

At that moment her brother, Joey, burst out of the front door and crashed right into Don, who reached out and grabbed the younger boy to steady him. "Whoa, easy there, kid. I might have to take you in for speeding in a restricted area."

"How many times do I have to tell you to watch where you're going?" Karen scolded. "Are you okay, Don?"

"Sure, no problem."

"This is my brother, Joey. Joey, this is Don Stanton."

Joey looked up and his eyes grew round. His mouth dropped open. "Don *Stanton?* Don Stanton from the *Sevilles?*

"Yeah, that's me."

"Wow! I heard you guys play in the park last summer! You're really super!"

"Well, thanks. Glad you liked us."

"You never told me you knew *Don Stanton.*" Joey gave his sister the most admiring look she had ever gotten from him. "I can't believe it! My sister knows Don Stanton! Hey, are you going to go out with him or something?"

"Joey!" Karen went red from embarrassment. She turned to Don, who seemed to think it was all very funny. "I'm sorry about this little beast, Don. If you just ignore him, maybe he'll go away." She glared at Joey.

Don shrugged. "Oh, that's cool—I have a ten-year-old sister *and* a seven-year-old brother. Believe me, I know what it's like. Every time they see me with a girl, they're all over me." He looked down at Joey, who showed no signs of leaving, but was staring at Don in awe.

Finally, Don ruffled Joey's hair and said, "Well, anyway, I'd better be going. So Karen, I'll see you. When I work this song out, I'll be in touch. Bye."

"Bye, Don."

"Take it easy, Joey."

"So long."

As Don drove off, Joey exclaimed, "Boy, wait'll I tell Petie Mears I met Don Stanton! Is he gonna be jealous! *Don Stanton* drove my sister home!

Holy cats!" He dashed away to share his news with his friends.

Karen let herself in the front door. From the kitchen, her mother called, "Karen? Is that you, dear?"

"It's me, Mom."

"How was your day?"

"Pretty good. My poem's in the *Clarion*." She walked into the kitchen, where her mother was reading a newspaper. "Want to see it?"

"Oh, honey, I'd love to." Mrs. Gillespie put aside the paper she'd been looking at. "Did you walk home from school?"

"Actually, I got a lift."

"Oh? Who from?"

"A boy I know. You haven't met him."

"Well, that was nice of him."

"Yes. It was. He's a nice boy."

With some surprise, Karen realized that he was.

Chapter Five

On Friday night Karen went over to Gwen's house. They made a huge bowl of popcorn and settled down in Gwen's room to watch the first of two movies they had rented. It was an old beach-party film from the sixties which they found hilarious.

Afterwards, Gwen was on her bed, lying flat on her back with her feet propped up against the wall. She dropped kernels of popcorn into her mouth.

Karen pressed the rewind button on the VCR, saying, "Our folks grew up on these movies. Can you believe it? They are so *bizarre!*"

Gwen giggled and said, "Can you see your mom in one of those beehive hairdos? Or your dad wearing those shorts or doing one of those dances? The sweet potato or whatever it was?"

Karen grabbed a handful of popcorn. "I found this old album of pictures from when they were in college. My dad had hair down to his shoulders and a big, droopy mustache! *My dad!* And my mother wore these funny old rimless glasses. She wore her hair real long and straight, and they *both* wore headbands!"

Gwen chewed her popcorn and tried to picture

it. "It's just too weird," she finally said. "You want to watch *Bog Monster*? It's supposed to be pretty good."

"Maybe a little later. So...how's things with Phil?"

Gwen smiled and sighed. "We studied together last night at his place. Karen, I'm so *happy*! Sometimes I think I'm going to wake up and it'll all have been a dream. And the amazing thing is," Gwen went on, swinging around to a sitting position on the bed, "we actually *did* study! And I think I finally began to understand a little trigonometry! Phil's really good at it, and he got me to where it made sense. I think I'm in love."

Karen broke the silence.

"Jeff and I are going to the movies tomorrow night," Karen said. "I took your advice, Gwen, and am giving him a second chance."

"Great!" Her friend smiled.

"But the funny thing is, I keep thinking about Don Stanton. Isn't that crazy? I hardly know the guy, and yet he seems to keep popping into my life. Did I tell you he gave me a ride home from school yesterday?"

"No, you didn't. Tell me everything!"

Gwen looked as if she might explode with excitement as Karen told her about Don's apology and his writing music for her lyrics.

"Didn't I tell you you'd make beautiful music together?" Gwen exclaimed when Karen had finished. "You're certainly coming out of your shell this year, Karen. Two good-looking, eligible guys interested in you at the same time. Unbelievable!" Gwen let out a long sigh.

46

"Hold on a minute, Gwen. No one said Don Stanton was interested in me. It's my lyrics he's after. Don't jump to conclusions."

"Nonsense." Gwen dismissed her friend's doubts with a wave of her hand.

"I don't know if I can handle all this anyway. I wish I could be calm and cool around boys—like you, Gwen. At the dance last week you were so relaxed."

Gwen gave Karen a lopsided grin. "You think I was relaxed that night? I was *paralyzed*! Here is this adorable boy who I've been wanting to notice me for months! And finally he asks me out, and all I could think of was, don't let me come off like a dim bulb! Don't let him find me boring! I wasn't relaxed at all, Karen—I was scared stiff!"

Karen stared. "But...but you were having so much fun!"

"Oh sure, we had fun. But even when I was laughing on the outside, I was *shaking* inside. See— you think that you're a geek with boys and that I'm not. The difference between us is that I can hide my being afraid better than you can."

Karen was amazed. "But I just thought—"

"I *know* what you just thought," sighed Gwen. "You thought that no girl ever got scared about boys except Karen Gillespie." She stood up suddenly, looking almost angry. "You know, for a smart girl, you are so...so *dumb* about some things."

"But...but how do you hide it? Why is it that when I get nervous I just freeze, and stand there like a lump, but you can talk and joke and dance and look like there's nothing wrong?"

Gwen squatted down in front of Karen and said, "Maybe it's because I've had lots of practice. Why do you think I make jokes? Because I found out that people like you when you do that. Remember when we were in fifth grade, and I was so skinny you could almost see through me in a strong light? I found out that when you do funny, goofy things, people laugh with you. And that's a lot better than having them laugh *at* you."

"You never told me any of this before. How come?"

Gwen shrugged. "I don't know. Maybe I just assumed you knew. You're the smart one, right?"

Karen went over and turned off the VCR. "I guess I'm not that smart in some ways. I mean, I could tell Jeff and I were uptight the other night, but it looked like you two were just having a ball."

"Don't you believe it. I felt like I was taking some kind of test. I hate olives on pizza. What if Phil *loves* olives on his pizza? I think football is dumb and boring. What if Phil thinks it's the greatest thing ever? What if he hates going to the beach, one of my favorite things in the whole world? See what I mean?"

"Yeah, I guess."

"Now, getting back to Don Stanton. Why didn't you tell me about him today at lunch?" Gwen looked both hurt and puzzled.

Karen picked up a fuzzy pink puppy from Gwen's stuffed-animal collection and gave it a hug. "I didn't tell you because I knew you'd get all crazy about it. He only said that because he felt bad about what happened at the dance and he wanted to make me feel better."

Gwen knelt on the bed and grabbed Karen's shoulders. "Don't you understand? He *likes* you!"

"What are you talking about?"

"He *likes* you! He didn't *have* to drive you home! He didn't *have* to compliment your poem!"

"Well, it wasn't a long drive—"

"Karen, read my lips. *He…likes…you.* Don't you understand? Why do you think he asked for your opinion of his songs in the first place? If he thought you were just a zero, he could've just stopped in the cafeteria or the hall one day and said, 'Sorry about the other night,' and that would've been that!"

"Well…I guess…maybe he likes my writing… *maybe.*"

Gwen threw up her hands and looked up at the ceiling in disgust. "No, *no*, NO! I mean, yes, he likes your writing, but that's not the point! He likes *you*! He's *interested* in you!"

Karen leaned back against the wall and crossed her arms. "Now, wait a minute. We're talking about Don Stanton. *Don Stanton,* who could go out with just about any girl in school. You're telling me he's interested in *me*? Are those new contact lenses messing up your brain?"

"I'm telling you, he likes you! He's going to write music and you're going to write the words. Soon you'll start making records and you'll go together. And when you're a big star and you have sports cars and swimming pools, I just hope you remember who told you so!" Gwen was jumping with enthusiasm.

"I promise, and you'll be able to swim in my pools and drive my cars any time you want." Karen smiled and shrugged her shoulders. "Let's see that other movie."

Karen slept late on Saturday morning and lazed around the house. The phone rang at about noon and was picked up downstairs.

"Karen!" her father called. "Honey! Phone for you!"

"Okay, coming. Who is it?"

"I don't know. It's a boy."

There were only two boys who could be calling her, and she secretly hoped it was Don. She picked up the upstairs extension. "I've got it up here, Daddy. You can hang up."

"Hello?" she said into the phone.

"Hi, Karen. This is Don Stanton."

"Oh! Hi." Karen felt a rush of excitement. She quickly took the phone into her room and shut the door.

"So...how are you?"

"Fine, thanks."

"I hope this isn't a bad time to call or anything."

"Oh no, it's okay. Everybody's up, I mean."

"I wanted to talk to you. I mean, I wanted to let you know, about that poem?"

Karen realized that she was squeezing the phone tight and tried to relax. "Yes?"

"Well, I was messing around with it yesterday, and I was up half the night with it. I wrote some music for it that sounds pretty good."

"Great!"

"So I was wondering, would you be interested in hearing it?"

"Sure! I'd love to."

"Fantastic. I tell you what—we're having a band rehearsal tomorrow afternoon and I was going to take them through it. Want to come?"

"Uh, well, yes! I'd like to."

"Fantastic! You understand, it'll sound pretty rough—the band hasn't heard it yet, and I just have the melody and the basic chords written down. I mean, there's no arrangement or anything."

"I understand."

"So you shouldn't expect too much, right away anyway."

"Oh, that's all right. Is it okay if I bring a friend?"

There was a pause on the other end of the line. "Who?"

"Gwen Morgan. She's my best friend and she really loves the Sevilles."

"Oh! Sure, no problem. Bring her along. We practice in our basement—my folks converted it into a studio for us. It's at Forty-nine Sycamore Place. Can you get there on your own, or should I pick you up?"

"No, that's all right. It's pretty close to here. I can get there on my own."

"Okay, then. We start at two o'clock, but we'll be going through some old stuff until three. Oh, and Karen?"

"Yes?"

"You're right, your lyrics are better than the old-hat stuff I was writing. Well, see you tomorrow."

"Bye." Karen hung up and put the phone on the floor by her bed. She lay back and stared up at the ceiling while her thoughts spun around and her heart raced. *Is it possible? Is this really happening?* She sat up abruptly and reached for the phone.

She dialed Gwen's number.

"Hello?" came Gwen's voice after a few rings.

"Hi, it's me."

"Oh, hi! What—"

"Don Stanton just called. He's written music to my poem."

"Hah! I *told* you! I was right! You're going to be rich and famous and—"

"Slow down, and listen for a minute. He asked me if I wanted to come to a Sevilles rehearsal tomorrow afternoon and hear it, and I asked him if it would be all right if you came along."

"Why'd you do that? Bad idea, Karen."

"What are you talking about?"

"You don't bring a girlfriend along on a date. It's like having a chaperone or something."

"Gwen, this is not a date, it's a band rehearsal. The whole band will be there, and maybe other people too. I just thought, since you were the one who kept telling me to show him my stuff, that maybe you'd want to be the first to hear the results."

"Terrific! Uh, what time is the rehearsal tomorrow? Not too early, I hope, 'cause Phil and I are going out tonight."

"Tonight!" Karen cried. "I almost forgot. I have a date with Jeff tonight."

"Two days, two dates," Gwen teased. "I'm finding it hard to feel very sorry for you, Karen. Your social life is becoming a regular whirlwind."

"Come on, Gwen. Be serious. How can I handle this? Is it fair to go out with two different guys at once? Oh, what am I saying? This isn't even a date with Don anyway. Gwen, you're my best friend."

Karen was getting desperate. "I need some advice. Help!"

Gwen smiled at her friend's hysterical tone. "Okay, calm down. You've already made a date with Jeff to go to the movies. So go. It wouldn't be fair to cancel at the last minute. And one date doesn't mean you're going to marry the guy. Then if you still feel the same way about Jeff—and Don—you can handle it then. In the meantime, enjoy it!"

"You're sure?" Karen sounded a little calmer.

"Yes. So I'll see you tomorrow at two-thirty."

"Have fun with Phil tonight."

"Oh, we will! We're going to Playland. And Karen, good luck tonight."

Karen replaced the phone in the upstairs hall and came downstairs in a happy daze. *Of course* Gwen was completely wrong about Don's being interested in her as a girl. But even so, he *was* interested in her as a writer, and tomorrow she was really going to hear a song that she had written!

But tonight, she had a date with Jeff. Karen sighed. What was she going to wear?

Chapter Six

"So how'd it go last night?" Gwen asked when Karen showed up at her door on Sunday afternoon.

"Jeff's a sweet guy, the movie was nice, but there were definitely no fireworks," Karen said with a sigh as she plopped down on Gwen's living-room sofa. "I'm going to have to tell him the truth. He seems to like me very much." Karen sighed again.

"Boy, is life complicated," Gwen said. "Hey, not a bad outfit, by the way," she added, noticing Karen's black jeans and soft black sweater. "Could use a little more color, but not bad at all."

Karen flushed with embarrassment and pleasure. She had purchased a pair of jeans similar to the ones Gwen had lent her for the dance. And she was pleased her friend had noticed. The sweater was a Christmas present she had never bothered to wear before.

"Thanks." Karen smiled. "I have a good teacher."

Gwen herself had on designer jeans and a brightly colored ski sweater. She grabbed a coat from the hall closet. "Let's go."

As they walked the few blocks to the Stantons', Karen asked, "So how was Playland?"

"Oh, it was so fantastic! We rode the Hurricane five times, and I didn't get sick. And it turns out that Phil and I are both bumper-car freaks, and later we went to a club where they had dancing. It was fabulous."

Mr. Stanton let them in when they arrived. As he led them through the attractive, sunny living room, they could hear the sound of the band from below, surprisingly muffled, with a heavy rhythmic pulse they felt under their feet.

In the kitchen, he pointed to a set of stairs leading down to the basement. "There you are, girls. At the foot of the stairs, go through the door on the left. They're all down there. Just follow your ears."

As they went down, the music got increasingly louder. When they opened the door, the volume washed over them. The band was going through an oldie. And while the amps weren't turned all the way up, it was easily loud enough to fill a room many times the size of this one. Clearly, the Stantons had done a good job of insulating the studio and allowing the people upstairs to go on with their lives, even while the Sevilles were rocking away down here. The floors, walls, and ceiling were covered in heavy, sound-absorbing material, and the door to the stairs was extra-thick and heavy.

There were five members of the Sevilles: a drummer, a keyboard player, two guitarists, and Don on bass. Their instruments, amplifiers, speakers, and cables filled up a lot of the room. Karen was not happy to discover that she and Gwen weren't the only guests at this rehearsal. Standing in front of the band and dancing to the music were Jennifer McSwain and her friend Tina Heath. They were both very dressed up. Tina, as usual, had on elaborate makeup, featuring blue eye shadow, lots of mascara, and vivid red lipstick, Karen suddenly felt like Cinderella *before* the ball. It didn't matter how she tried, she couldn't compete with girls who looked like that. Don wouldn't even notice her new outfit.

Gwen turned and said something, but with the band thundering a few feet away, Karen couldn't make out a word. She gestured to Gwen that she hadn't been able to hear, and Gwen leaned in and shouted at the top of her voice. Unfortunately, the band came to a stop just in time for everyone to hear Gwen say, "...like she learned makeup at clown school."

"Hey! Glad you could make it!" With a welcoming smile, Don unplugged his bass and put it down. Jennifer and Tina appeared to find the new arrivals a most *un*welcome surprise.

Karen's ears were ringing and she knew her face was growing red from the attention. She wished she at least had worn some serious makeup. But there was nothing to be done but live with her choice now.

"Don, this is my friend, Gwen Morgan."

"Hi, Gwen."

"Hi, I just want to say that I think you're terrific."

"Thanks."

Don gestured toward the band. "Come on and meet the rest of the group. This is Bobby Mitchell on drums." Bobby, a cheerful, husky guy with blond hair cut very short, waved a drumstick in greeting.

"The guy on synthesizer is Ed Fletcher." Ed was all in black, with dark shades on his eyes. He was pale and skinny, and he nodded, expressionless.

"Paul Turnbull plays rhythm guitar and mouth harp, and our lead guitarist is Fred Knight. We call him 'Fingers.'" Paul was a muscular six-footer with curly brown hair, and Fred had a face full of freckles and red hair that was mostly covered by a baseball cap.

"Guys, this is Karen Gillespie and Gwen Morgan. I guess you girls must know Jennifer and Tina."

"I guess we must," said Gwen.

Tina leaned over and whispered something to Jennifer, who nodded and giggled. Don frowned at them and went over to pick some music off the top of an amplifier.

He took it over to the synthesizer, where Ed shifted over to give Don room to sit at the keyboard. Don sat down and spread out his music. He played a few chords and fussed with the music some more. He looked a little nervous.

"Okay," he said, "Karen wrote this, and I really liked the words. It ought to be a dynamite number. I'll just run through it by myself, then we can work out some kind of arrangement for it." He counted off a slow tempo and began to sing Karen's lyric:

"What's the difference
    What clothes I choose to wear,
    How I want to keep my hair,
    If my bedroom isn't neat,
    Whether I watch what I eat,

The world just goes its own way,
Makes no difference what I do or say.

"It makes no difference,
In a game that has no rules,
What's the point of books or schools,
Do as they say, not as they do,
If they say so, it must be true—
The world just goes its own way
Makes no difference what I do or say..."

Don's music fits the words real well, Karen thought. It had a slow, intense beat, giving a melancholy feel to the lyrics. He understood her poem perfectly, Karen realized. The music complemented it. He saw beyond the words into the feeling behind them. It made Karen shine with excitement. It was meant to be a song.

Gwen smiled at Karen in approval, and the other band members were nodding happily. Bobby added a drum riff that fit in perfectly. The rhythm guitarist looked at the music over Don's shoulder and came in after the second verse. And by the final verse, the lead guitarist was filling in, adding harmony vocals here and there.

Karen had never listened to a group of musicians learn a number before, and to her it was like magic. It came together so quickly, and when it ended, she was speechless. The song was beautiful, yet sad, and left Karen feeling both elated and melancholy.

Don swiveled in his seat to look at Karen after he finished playing. Their eyes locked for a moment. Then he said abruptly, "Of course, that's just a rough idea, you understand. Once we've had a chance to work with it a little, it's going to be a lot tighter."

"Oh, no," Karen assured him. "I think it's *perfect*. Just the way it is now."

Ed, the keyboard player, spoke up. "Dynamite song, man." He looked curiously at Karen. "*You* wrote that, huh?" She nodded. "You don't look the type. But you never know." Ed reached over to poke Don's shoulder. "Hey, man, get outta that chair and let me try something. How's this sound?" And he played a bluesy line, using the chord sequence that Don had written. The others picked up on it immediately.

The lead guitarist said, "Wait a minute, hold it!" They stopped and turned to him. "How's this for an intro? I start with a lick like this—" He played a piece that led beautifully into the rhythmic backing that Ed had come up with. "— and then everyone comes in *here*."

Karen whispered to Gwen, who was bouncing up and down in place, "Can you believe this?" And Gwen mouthed the words "I told you so" and winked.

"All right, everybody, let's take the whole thing from the top," said Don. "Don't let it get any faster, we don't want to lose any words. It's your opening, Fingers, so you set the tempo. Okay, ready?"

They ran through the whole song again. It was different this time—the guitarists added little ornamental fills, and there was more harmony vocalizing. Between the two verses, there was a lead guitar solo. It came to a delicate conclusion with a slow fade. The room was silent for a few seconds.

Bobby smiled broadly from behind his drum kit. "What a ballad," he said softly. "That's some song."

Don unslung his bass and walked over to Karen. He took her hands in his. "Congratulations. I think we have a winner."

They smiled at each other. "It's really wonderful," she said.

Don let go of her hands and replied, "It can be better. Once we've worked out all the backing vocals and figured out where to put the little fills and stings...well, you just wait. Jennifer, what did you think?"

Jennifer and Tina had been sitting on a couple of beat-up folding chairs, looking gloomy at not being the center of attention. At Don's question, they brightened. Jennifer gave Don her most dazzling smile. "I think it's super, Donny, just like *all* your songs."

Tina put a hand to her elaborately layered hair. "I just *adore* all your writing, Donny." Neither girl paid any attention to Karen.

Gwen glared at them and said, "It isn't *Don's* song, it's Don and *Karen's* song."

"Absolutely," agreed Don. He looked over at Jennifer. "I can't claim all the credit for this one. Karen wrote the lyrics."

Jennifer looked scornful. "That's true, Donny. But without your music, it wouldn't be anything. *You* made it a song."

"That's right, Donny," chimed in Tina. "You could make a good song out of a...a shopping list, if you wanted."

Don let out a laugh. "Thanks for the vote of

confidence, but I don't think so."

"Well, it's true," Jennifer insisted. "And what's a song without music and a great voice to sing it!"

Don looked thoughtful for a moment. "A singing voice," he murmured, turning to give Karen an appraising look. "Maybe she *can* sing," he said with a smile.

Karen heard Jennifer and Tina snickering in the corner, and the old, uncomfortable heat crept up into her face. Don took a step toward her. *"Can* you?"

"Can I what?" she asked faintly.

"Sing. Can you sing? A couple of times we've talked about finding a girl singer to work with us."

"So we don't have to listen to Don's singing all the time," put in Eddie, deadpan.

Don wouldn't let it go. "Karen? *Can* you sing?"

Wordlessly she shrugged her shoulders, her eyes fixed on the floor. "I sing when I'm alone, but I've never studied, or even joined the school chorus."

"I'm not asking if you've studied or have a trained voice," Don went on. "But can you carry a tune? Do you enjoy it?"

Karen shrugged again. "I guess so."

"A lot of women songwriters sing their own stuff, you know. And it would give our band a new dimension. If you could—"

"Well, I couldn't" Karen interrupted. "I couldn't get up on a stage in front of a lot of people, with all those bright lights and everyone looking at me...I just couldn't. No."

"It's really not that big a deal," Don said quietly. "Karen, listen. Everybody's nervous the first time they appear in front of a crowd. *I* sure was. But you get over it. I think you *could*, if you gave it a shot."

Paul, the rhythm guitarist, tapped Don on the shoulder. "Hey, cool it, Don. If she doesn't want to, she doesn't want to."

Don nodded impatiently. "I don't want to force her to do anything. I only figured, if she gives it a try, like at a rehearsal, maybe she'll be surprised."

Speaking just loud enough for Karen to hear, Jennifer said to Tina, "Wouldn't you simply *love* to see her sing with a band?"

"It'd make a great comedy act," Tina whispered back.

Gwen gave the two girls an angry stare, then turned to Don. "Why don't you just drop the subject for now, okay?"

Don raised his hands in mock surrender. "Okay, okay. I just had a feeling about it. It was worth a try, but—"

"I have to go," Karen murmured so softly that Don could barely hear her, and ran to the door. She pulled it open and went out and up the steps rapidly.

"Hey!" said Don. He started after her. "Karen, what—"

Gwen stepped in front of him. "I think I better go with her. You stay here." She glared one last time at Jennifer and Tina, and followed her friend.

Outside the house, Gwen overtook Karen, who was walking with her head down and her hands in her pockets.

"Karen? Are you okay?"

Karen didn't respond, but kept walking. Gwen stayed with her, watching her with concern.

"Karen? *Please*, talk to me. Come on, what's going on? You should be flattered, you know."

Karen stopped, but wouldn't speak or look up for a long moment. She took a few deep, shaky breaths, then raised her eyes to meet Gwen's.

"I'm sorry," she said.

Gwen was mystified. "Sorry? Sorry for what?"

"I just had to get out of there. Jennifer and Tina were laughing at me, and I felt like a fool. I couldn't open my mouth, and I couldn't think, and I had to get out. I feel like a dope."

Gwen put her arm around Karen's shoulders.

"You shouldn't pay any attention to Jennifer and Tina. They're just a couple of spoiled brats who couldn't stand it that Don was paying more attention to you than he was to them."

"Why did he keep on insisting? It's a ridiculous idea. No wonder those girls were laughing. The guys in the band would've laughed too, but they were too nice."

Gwen thought in silence for a few minutes. "I guess Don didn't think it was such a ridiculous idea. Otherwise, why *would* he ask?"

"I don't know. It must have been some kind of bad joke. Ha, ha!"

Gwen began to chew on her lower lip as they walked—a sign, Karen knew, that she was deep in thought. Then she came to a dead halt on the sidewalk. "Nope. He asked you because he likes you."

Karen's mouth fell open as she stared at her friend. "That's totally crazy! He embarrassed me like that because he *likes* me?"

"He wasn't *trying* to embarrass you. Don't you see? Look." Gwen began to pace back and forth

63

across the width of the sidewalk as she explained.

"If he said, 'Maybe you could sing with the Sevilles' to almost any other girl in school, the girl would be *thrilled*. No matter if she could sing or not, whether she took it seriously or not. Because what he's *really* saying is, you'd look good up on stage with us. He spends a lot of time with his band. He'd *like* to spend a lot more time with you. If you started working with the band, then you would *have* to spend more time with him. See?

"Maybe it was wishful thinking, but he wasn't trying to make you look bad. He was really saying how much he liked you. And I also think it would be good for the band, too. Dress up the act. And he obviously loved your lyrics. *That's* why he brought up the idea of you singing, I think."

Gwen crossed her arms with a self-satisfied smile as she finished her explanation. Karen shook her head. "I know you want me to feel better, but I just can't believe it. If he likes me, why doesn't he ask me out?"

"Maybe he doesn't ask you for a date because he's shy."

"*Shy?* Get real! He always has girls hanging all over him, and he never seemed shy before."

"Well, he's not shy with *them*. But maybe he's shy with *you*."

"Why me?"

"Because he *likes* you," said Gwen triumphantly.

Karen burst out laughing and reached out and hugged Gwen tightly. They clung together for a few seconds. Karen realized that she felt a lot better. She was lucky to have a friend like Gwen.

"All right, all right, you win," she said. "Maybe

he likes me a little. Or at least *liked* me before I went running out of his house without a word. I'm going to tell you a secret, but you have to *swear* that you'll never tell anybody else."

"I swear."

"I really mean it. I've never told anybody."

"You can trust me. I won't say anything."

"Okay. Now don't laugh. I'd *love* to be a singer. I've dreamed about performing my own songs. It's my fantasy. But that's all it'll ever be."

"Why are you so sure?"

"Oh, come on, Gwen! When I try to dance, I freeze because I think everyone's looking at me. When I'm with some other kids and they're joking around, I get tongue-tied because I think everybody's looking at me. What do you think would happen if I got up on a stage, in front of a huge crowd of people, *knowing* that everybody is looking at me? Forget it. It's just a dream."

"Well, maybe you're right." They had arrived in front of Gwen's house. "But you'll never know unless you try."

Karen smiled. "I'll think about it. And thanks for coming with me today."

"I was glad to. By the way, that's a great song."

The two girls hugged again. They separated, and Karen turned to go. Gwen called out after her, "Can I say one more thing to you?"

Karen stopped and turned around. "Sure."

Gwen slowly walked up to her friend with a very serious look on her face.

"He likes you."

Karen hurled a pile of autumn leaves at her as Gwen raced to her front door.

Chapter Seven

On Monday, Karen walked to school with the beginning of a poem running through her mind. The idea had come to her that morning while she was brushing her teeth. She hoped that the words might turn into a song lyric once they were completed:

Like a magnet does to steel,
Like a flower does to a bee,
Like catnip does to kittens, babe,
That's what you do to me,
It's called attraction...

That's what she'd call it: "Attraction." She'd try to work on it during study hall. Maybe she would give it to Don when...when she got up the nerve to talk to him again.

Jeff Whitman was sitting on the front steps of the school as she arrived. His presence startled her. She'd all but forgotten their uneventful date Saturday night—Don and the band were occupying all her thoughts.

"Hi."

"Hello, Karen. How was the rest of your weekend? Get all your work done?"

"It was okay. How's the next *Clarion* coming along?"

"All right, I guess. Look, Karen, I was wondering. I had a nice time Saturday night.... How about a movie next weekend? There's some old Charlie Chaplin stuff in town."

Karen looked around. They still had ten minutes before homeroom. People were streaming into the building, chattering, laughing, thinking, paying no particular attention to them. She didn't feel up to handling this, but Jeff was a decent guy and deserved the truth from her. She pointed to one of the stone benches on either side of the main doors and said, "Let's sit down for a second."

When they were seated, she took a deep breath and turned to face him. "Jeff, I'm sorry. But I don't think it's such a great idea for me to go out with you again. I like you and I think you're a good friend, but..." Her voice trailed away. This was one of the hardest things she'd ever had to do.

Jeff looked away. "Oh," he said very softly. "Can I ask you... is it because I did something wrong?"

"No, it's nothing like that. I think it's just me. It isn't fair not to tell you that I only want to be friends. I like talking to you, and I want to work on the paper with you. I hope we still can. But... that's all. It wouldn't be right to let you think any different. But thank you for asking me. Okay?"

"Okay." He stood up, not looking at her. "Well ...see you." He walked quickly away and through the doors.

She sat and watched him leave. That was over.

Karen hoped he didn't feel too hurt. She collected her purse and books and joined the crowd on its way to begin the school week.

The day went pretty well, for a Monday, and she actually enjoyed her English class, getting very caught up in a discussion of Emily Dickinson's poetry. She actually earned a pleasant smile from Ms. Davis. Once or twice in the course of the morning she thought back to what had happened the day before at band rehearsal and a feeling of embarrassment and excitement would wash over her. It took all her concentration to keep her mind on her classes.

She was on the lunch line at the cafeteria when she sensed someone was staring at her. She turned, and there was Don.

"I'd like to talk to you," he said.

She was aware of the many students surrounding them. "Now? Here?"

"We could have lunch outside, if you want." He held up a brown bag. "I have enough here to share with you. My mom always gives me enough to feed a starving army. There're a couple of sandwiches, fruit, potato salad, homemade brownies..."

"All right. How do you stay so skinny with a mother like that?"

"I can usually find a starving army to share with."

She stacked her tray back in the pile and stepped out of the line. As they walked through the cafeteria toward the hall, Karen spotted Gwen and Phil sitting together. Gwen waved and winked at her, giving her a thumbs-up signal. Karen mouthed a silent "See you later" and waved back.

"Donny! I saved you a seat!" Jennifer McSwain called out as they passed her and her group.

"Sorry, not today," he called back as they walked on. Out of the corner of her eye, Karen saw a hurt look on Jennifer's pretty face as she watched them leave the room.

It was an unusually warm autumn day, so there were a few groups of kids sitting on the steps. Don found a spot not too close to anybody else.

"I hope you don't mind coming out here," he said. "You want a sandwich? Help yourself."

Karen looked into the large, well-packed bag and pulled out an apple. "No, this is fine," she replied.

"I'm sorry about yesterday. I didn't mean to put you on the spot. I just wasn't thinking."

Karen shook her head. "You don't have anything to be sorry for. I'm the one who behaved badly. I don't know why I ran out like that. I felt terrible afterwards."

"I told off Jennifer, and Tina too. I think they actually felt a little ashamed."

"Really?" Karen found it hard to believe.

"Oh, I know you're not crazy about them, but they're really not so bad. Jennifer can be very sweet, sometimes. I think her parents treat her like a little princess, so she's pretty spoiled. When she can't have everything her own way, she can't handle it real well. Maybe she'll learn." He took a bite out of a sandwich. "Maybe one day she'll even realize that I hate being called Donny."

Karen nibbled on her apple. "About yesterday, I wanted to tell you…" She hesitated. "It's going to sound so stupid…"

"No it isn't."

"Well, when you asked if I could sing, I—I just thought that you were, like, making a joke. I mean, me doing anything in front of a lot of people is a comical thought."

Don frowned. "You think I'd make fun of you that way?"

"Oh, I know now you wouldn't. After I talked with Gwen for a few minutes, I knew that I'd been overreacting. I felt awful and knew that you must have felt bad, too. It was *my* fault, really. So I should apologize to *you*."

"I tell you what—I won't feel sorry if you won't either." He stuck out his hand. "Shake on it?"

"All right." Karen took the offered hand and shook it. His long fingers were callused at the tips from playing the bass.

"Great! You want anything else to eat?" He held out the bag.

"No, I'm fine."

"Listen, if you have any more possible song material, I want to see it."

"Well..." She leafed through her notebook and pulled out what she had written of "Attraction."

"It isn't finished yet, but there's enough to give you an idea." She watched him anxiously as he read it through. He finished and looked up with a smile.

"You know one reason you're a really talented songwriter?" He waved the sheet of paper. "It's your sense of rhythm. This has a dynamite natural rhythm written into it. So did 'The Difference.' Even with no music, the words just kind of dance on the paper when you read them. That's one

reason why I thought that you might be a singer—
you've got that beat inside you."

"I do?" Karen was startled and a little embarrassed.

"Oh, lots of people have it—in their bodies. But
not so many can do it with words. That's why I..."
He stared at her closely. "Are you *sure* you can't
sing?" He'd finished his sandwich, and started on
a brownie.

"I'm pretty sure."

"Karen, are you sure it's because you *can't*, and
not because you *won't* sing?" Don gave her an
intense look.

"I don't know...maybe." Karen shrugged.

"Aha!" He pointed at her with a paper napkin.
"I bet you've never tried."

"I just couldn't do it, Don. I'm sorry, but I
couldn't sing in front of a lot of people. I'd get all
panicky and freeze up. I'd be awful."

"I see." He nodded. "You have stage fright. A lot
of entertainers have that and it sort of wears off
after a while."

"It's not just stage fright, though. It's more like
'center-of-attention fright.' That's much worse."

"Why? I don't get it."

Karen wrapped her apple core in a napkin as she
tried to explain. "I'm afraid of looking silly or...
out of place in front of people. If it was just stage
fright, then I could just stay away from performing and everything would be okay. But I feel uncomfortable in lots of places. Like at a dance or
a party. I get so self-conscious, and that just makes
it worse. So I usually just avoid parties and dances
and things like that." She couldn't believe she was

telling this to Don, but he was easy to talk to and seemed to understand.

"But couldn't you just *not* think about yourself doing something, and just *do* it? I bet it'd be a lot easier for you if you didn't think so much."

"Oh, I *know* it would be!" She leaned forward eagerly. "I wish we were given brains with on/off switches; but I can't find the right switch, so I guess I'll go through life feeling embarrassed and awkward a lot." A look of surprise passed over Karen's face. "Usually I feel uncomfortable talking about myself like this. Except with Gwen. Then I tried talking about it with Jeff when we went to the School Spirit Dance, and *he* got uncomfortable."

"Well, *I'm* not." Don handed her the sheet of notebook paper with the unfinished lyrics. "Could you have this finished by Wednesday?"

"Wednesday?" Karen gave it a moment's thought. "I guess so, sure."

"Okay." Don collected the trash from their lunch and tossed it into a nearby wastebasket. "If you don't have any plans, could you come over to my place Wednesday night?"

"Umm...all right. I'll bring the lyrics."

"Terrific! And I'd like to try something—only if it's okay with you."

"What?"

"I'd like to hear you sing a little." He held up a hand as she started to protest. "It'll just be you and me in the studio. No other Sevilles, no friends. Just us. If you sound like a sick kitten, we'll stop. Okay? Come on, it'll be fun."

"Why? What's so important about hearing me sing?"

He shrugged. "Oh, I don't know. I just have this feeling that there's music in you. And I think we can try to bring it out. If it sounds ridiculous, we'll stop, and no one will ever know. What do you say?"

"Well, I guess so."

"All right! Seven-thirty Wednesday, and bring the new song." They got up to return inside. "Hey, it was nice having lunch with you."

"Thanks for the apple. And I'm glad we talked. Bye, Don."

"See you."

At the end of the day, Karen ran into Gwen and Phil on the front steps. "Hi!" said Gwen brightly. "You walking home? Wait a minute and I'll go with you. Phil's got a meeting with the basketball team."

"We start practice next week," said Phil, miming a shot with an imaginary ball.

"Phil's going to get his letter this season," announced Gwen proudly, hooking her arm through his.

"I would've got it last year, but I sprained my ankle. Well, see you, babe."

Gwen squeezed his hand. "I'll phone you tonight after dinner. Bye." She slung her bookbag over her shoulder, and the two girls went down the steps.

"I'm not going to say, 'I told you so'—but I *did*, didn't I!" Gwen looked very smug.

"Told me so about what?" asked Karen innocently.

"Oh, cut it out! By the way, when the two of you

walked out of the cafeteria, you should have seen the look on Jennifer's face. She was like a little girl who just found out there's no Santa Claus."

"Don't gloat. She just likes him a lot, and he isn't really interested in her."

"Now isn't that just too bad!"

"Don says that she's just used to getting her own way, and doesn't know what to do when she doesn't. I could almost feel sorry for her."

Gwen switched the bookbag to her other shoulder and glanced curiously at Karen.

"Uh-huh. Is that all you and Don did at lunch— talk about Jennifer?"

"Of course not! We talked about other things. Like music, and songwriting, stuff like that."

"And..." prompted Gwen impatiently.

"You want to hear every little detail? I didn't take any notes."

"Oh, that's all right. If you don't want to confide in your best friend, who tells you absolutely *everything* that is on her mind, and who is probably going to die of curiosity in three minutes, you don't have to. After all, I'm only the one who got you two together in the first place."

Karen stopped dead in the middle of an intersection. "Got us together? What are you talking about?"

"Who was it who told you to show him your poems? Wasn't that how it all began?"

"You did, but..."

"You don't have to thank me; it's what friends are for..."

"Gwen..."

"No, no, Karen, it's all right. Shut me out of

your life if you want to. I've done my little job, so just forget about poor old Gwen, the one who brought the two of you together."

"Will you stop? You keep saying you got us together, but we *aren't* together! I'll tell you what we talked about, and then you'll be disappointed because it's *boring*. Well, maybe not boring, but it certainly wasn't romantic, either."

"So *you* say. So tell me."

"He said that he was sorry if he'd embarrassed me at the rehearsal. He hadn't thought I'd react that way."

"*Told* you so," murmured Gwen, just loud enough for Karen to hear.

"And I told him that he hadn't done anything to feel sorry about, that I had misunderstood. And I showed him part of a new song I was working on, and he liked it. Then he asked me to come over to his studio Wednesday night."

"Is there a band rehearsal that night?"

"No."

"So, who's going to be there?" Gwen grinned slyly. "Just the two of you?"

"He wants to hear if I can sing at all, and with nobody else there, I won't get so uptight."

Gwen still had a grin on her face. "Oh, so he's interested in your *voice*? Right."

"He says that my writing has great rhythm in it, and that he has a hunch that I ought to be able to sing. And we'll look at the new song if I finish the words. That's all. No big romance."

"Karen—do you like him?"

"I think he's nice."

Gwen shook her head. "Come on! You know

what I mean, Karen. Do you?"

"I don't...he's...could we change the subject?"

"Why won't you even talk about it?"

Karen walked a while before answering.

"Because I don't want to start thinking about him that way. I'd like to have him for a friend. I feel easy with him, and, yes, you were right, he *does* like my writing."

But Karen didn't want to be just another one of the girls that were always hanging around him, hoping for a date. Also, what would happen if she decided she really liked him a lot, and it turned out that he wasn't interested in her at all—except as a writer? What then? It was better not to think about it. No sense getting her hopes up.

"Gwen, what would happen if you and Phil broke up?" she asked.

"Oh...I guess I'd cry a lot, and I'd feel awful for a while. Is that it? Are you afraid that could happen to you?"

"Well, wouldn't it?"

"Sure. But so what? Believe me, it's worth the risk."

"Maybe it is for you. I don't know if I'm ready to handle it."

Gwen laughed. "Do you think I asked myself if I was 'ready' to start going with Phil? It just happened. When it happens to you, then you'll find out if you're ready or not. See, there's nothing to think about. Personally, I think you're as 'ready' as I was."

Karen reached out and grabbed Gwen's hand. "It's confusing. I don't know, I guess I'm scared. I don't know *what* I feel. And I don't know what *he* feels. I'm glad you're always there to talk to, but I don't want to talk about Don and me. Not yet anyway."

They had reached Karen's house. Karen started up the front path. "See you later."

Gwen called out after her, "Want to meet for lunch tomorrow—or are you seeing Don again?"

Karen turned back and gave Gwen a mock scowl. "Save me a seat."

She let herself into the house, and she was suddenly surprised to realize how very much she was looking forward to Wednesday night.

Chapter Eight

When Karen rang the Stantons' doorbell on Wednesday, it was Don himself who let her in.

"Hi. Come on in."

"Thanks."

"Can I get you something? Cider? Cookies?"

"No, thanks, we just had dinner."

They went into the kitchen, where a girl sat at the table surrounded by colored paper, scissors, and glue. She had Don's light brown hair and similar facial features.

"Linda, say hi to Karen."

Linda studied Karen intently before saying a quiet, "Hi."

"Hi, Linda. What are you working on?"

"It's homework. For art. You cut up colored paper and stick it all together like a picture. It's called a collage."

Don peered closer at his sister's work. "It's looking pretty good, kiddo. Where's Mikey?"

"Upstairs, playing video games."

The back door opened and Mrs. Stanton walked into the kitchen, carrying a watering can. She was tall and athletic-looking, and she had on what was clearly her gardening outfit: faded jeans, plaid work shirt, and a pair of sandals.

"Mom," said Don, "this is Karen Gillespie. Karen, this is my mother."

"How do you do, Mrs. Stanton."

"Well, Karen, it's very nice to meet you." She gave her son a grin. "I've been hearing a lot about you lately. I understand you're quite a writer."

"Oh! Well, thank you."

"Mom, we'll be down in the studio if anyone calls," Don said, opening the basement door. "Come on, Karen."

"Okay. Nice meeting you, Mrs. Stanton. You too, Linda."

They clumped down the stairs, Don in the lead. "How old is your sister?" asked Karen.

"She's ten. Her fifth-grade teacher thinks she's pretty talented, so she gives her these special assignments."

He pulled open the heavy studio door and flipped on the lights. The room was less crowded than it had been on Sunday. Much of the band gear was either gone or packed away. The synthesizer was still sitting there. It didn't look like much—just a piano-type keyboard with a whole lot of knobs, dials, buttons, and red lights on it, sitting on four spindly collapsible legs. Don sat at the keyboard and flipped a switch to turn it on. He played a couple of chords.

"Did you bring that new song lyric?"

Karen took a couple of folded sheets of loose-leaf paper from her purse and handed them to him. He put them on top of the synthesizer and read through them quickly.

"Great!" He twisted a couple of knobs, flicked

a switch, and moved one slide control. A basic, rock-and-roll drum riff came out of the speakers. Don listened for a second and adjusted a control. The beat picked up slightly. Karen watched, fascinated, as Don swiveled to talk to her.

"That's a good basic tempo for it, I think." And he read the lyrics out loud, fitting them to the synthesizer's rhythm. "What do you say? That about right?"

"It sounds fine to me. What a great gadget this is!"

"Haven't you seen one of these before?" Don patted the top lovingly. "This is my baby. I do all my writing on it, and I use it for making arrangements. You can do so much with one of these things—and this is just a simple one. The really good, state-of-the-art ones can do anything. You don't even need a human being to play them anymore."

"Really?"

"Well, no, not quite. Not yet, anyway."

Using the same drumbeat, he played a short blues tune. As he played, he bent over the keys and swayed from side to side with the music. As he finished, with a couple of big, hammered fistfuls of notes, he turned off the rhythm.

"That's pretty," Karen said. "Did you write that?"

"Nobody wrote it. It's just a little blues thing. You know, just messing around with the basic blues chord sequence." He played the chords through for her. "See? That's the basis for all blues songs. Then, you take the chords and build on them." He demonstrated with a line of melody over the chords. "And that's it. The birth of the blues."

Flipping a few more switches, he played what sounded like a trumpet fanfare. *Ta-da.*

Karen was enthralled. She'd been thinking about this evening and had been really nervous on her way over. But now, she was too interested to remember to be nervous.

Don jumped up and unfolded a chair from against a wall, placing it down next to the keyboard. "Have a seat. Let's try something."

Karen sat, and Don resumed his place at the synthesizer alongside her.

"If you really want to be a songwriter," he said, "it's important to be able to sing. Even if you don't want to perform in public. That way, you'll find out that good poetry doesn't necessarily make a good song. Like, some words are hard to pronounce when you're singing fast. Or, say you have to hit a high note and hold it. Then it's better to use big, open vowel sounds, like this: Aaaaaaah!" Don sang the vowel, playing an accompaniment to himself.

"But it doesn't sound good if the note is on a thin vowel sound, like: Eeeeeeeeee! See what I mean?"

Karen nodded.

"Now that's the kind of stuff where it helps to be a singer too. So you don't wind up writing something that looks good on paper, but *sounds* terrible." He swung around on his seat to face Karen.

"Now I'm going to play a note, and you sing it. Just sing 'Aaaaaah' on that note. Okay? Then I'll play another one, and so on."

He played a note, and Karen came out with a timid, shaky, thin "Aaaah." He nodded encouragement and played another note. Gradually, she sang out a little louder. He went up the scale until he reached a note that was too high for her, and he did the same thing at the lower end.

"Well," he said afterwards, "you are definitely not tone deaf. And your vocal range isn't bad, either."

"Thank you."

"Now. Let's try singing a song. How about 'Mary Had a Little Lamb'?"

They went through "Mary Had a Little Lamb" and "Three Blind Mice" and some old familiar folk songs. Don would try different keys and give her little tips, like looking for the right places to breathe while singing. They tried slow ballads and then moved into up-tempo, rocking oldies. Don would occasionally sing along.

Karen had started off feeling very self-conscious and not a little foolish, but after a few songs she began to enjoy herself. The music and the words came together naturally. They finished off with one of the hottest contemporary hits, and when it ended, Karen was amazed to realize that she had been singing for almost an hour.

"Wow!" That was all Don had to say at first. They smiled at each other. "How's your throat? Feel okay? You gave it a real workout."

"Fine. How was I?"

"I have to tell you, I'm amazed. I mean, I had a feeling you could do it, but you're a lot better than I hoped. There's still a lot that you need to learn, but some of it you'd pick up with just a little training. So, what do *you* think?"

"What do *I*...I had no idea...it's so...I love

listening to music, and to actually be able to *do* it ...
it was...just..."

Don laughed. "Sounds like you enjoyed yourself."

"Oh! Yes, yes, it was wonderful! How did you
know I could do this?"

"I didn't *know*, exactly." He began to play
softly as he talked. "I had a feeling, that was all.
You have the words in you, and you have the beat.
So...I just had a hunch. Also, I was hoping you
could sing."

"Why?" said Karen softly, watching his hands
move over the keys.

"Well, for one thing, it's helpful to a songwriter,
like I said. For another thing...look, if you're not
too tired, would you like to try one more?"

"Sure! What?"

"Let's go for your song, 'The Difference.' We'll
go through it once real easy, so you can hear the
tune, and then we'll do it for real. And this time,
while you sing it, think about the words. Think
about how they make you feel, and let the feeling
come through your voice. All right?"

Karen remembered Don's melody easily enough
after the first run-through and sang with real
feeling the second time around. She tried for a
sound that was angry in some places, sad in others.
Then she pretty much stopped thinking altogether
and just sang.

As they finished the song, Karen was surprised
to hear clapping from behind them. In the doorway were Mrs. Stanton and Linda, applauding
happily.

"That was wonderful!" exclaimed Mrs. Stanton.

"I liked it a lot," Linda added.

Don gestured toward Karen. "*We* wrote it. Karen wrote the words."

Mrs. Stanton looked at her thoughtfully. "I think you have real talent, Karen."

"Thank you."

"I just came down here to let you know that Linda and I are having some hot apple cider. How would you like some? And a few oatmeal cookies?"

"Mom makes the best cookies ever!" said Linda.

"I'd love some," answered Karen, who realized that she was very thirsty.

"Well, I'll just put some on a tray, and you can come up for it whenever you like. Don, it's a school night, remember. Not too late."

"Right, Mom. Thanks."

Don stood up and stretched. "Come on in here," he said to Karen. They left the studio and crossed to the other half of the basement, which was fixed up as a den. There was a beat-up old couch, a few chairs, a TV, and some stereo equipment, along with a cabinet full of records, tapes, and CD's.

"Sit down and make yourself comfortable. I'll get the cider," said Don, who disappeared up the steps.

Moments later he was back carrying a large tray, on which were two steaming mugs of cider and a plateful of cookies. "Eat 'em while they're still warm. Linda's right—Mom makes great cookies."

Karen took a cookie and a mug and sat down on the couch while Don went over to the stereo and looked through the collection of records, tapes, and CD's. A pleasant cinnamon smell filled the room as she sipped from the mug. Don put on a

CD and chose a slightly frayed, overstuffed arm-chair. The music came on, sounding scratchy and thin, evidently from old recordings. A woman's voice sang out, strong and rich, even in the outdated recording. They listened quietly for a few minutes.

The song was a sad one. "Nobody wants you when you're down and out," sang the voice, which seemed to know all about it.

"Like it?" asked Don.

"Who *is* it?"

"Billie Holiday. She was an old-time blues singer. All this stuff is from around nineteen-thirty. But even though it's old she still sounds great, doesn't she?"

Karen nodded, fascinated and attracted by the beautiful voice out of the past, and by the song, which was sweet and sad.

"Listen to how she sings some notes," Don said, leaning forward and putting down his mug on an old coffee table. "You hear the way she doesn't always just hit a note and hold it, she sort of *bends* the note a little? And she doesn't just hit the beat, she sings *off* the beat. That's what gives it that 'blues' feeling, that's what makes it swing. You can learn a lot about singing from listening to her."

Karen smiled at Don. "Thanks for playing this for me."

"If you want, I can lend you a few things so you can listen at home." He went over to the cabinet and went through its shelves, pulling out a few records and tapes. "Listening to this stuff can teach you a lot about singing."

Karen leaned back, cupping the mug in both hands. She felt relaxed and comfortable. Yet at the same time she felt excited, as if a whole new world was being opened up to her. *Can I learn to do this? Is it possible?* Mrs. Stanton had said that she had talent. But maybe she was only being polite.

"Do you want to be a professional musician?" she asked him.

Don sat back down in his armchair and propped his feet up on the table. "I take lessons from a guy," he said. "He teaches me guitar and bass, and he also gives me lessons in theory and composing. He's really *good*. I asked him once about making music my profession. And he said, 'Take my advice: stay in school, get your education, go to college. Because there are a million kids who want to be professional musicians and most of them won't make it. It's better to have some kind of choice.'

"So, I'm following his ideas. I figure, maybe it'll happen, but if it doesn't, then there'll be other possibilities. Also, I could suddenly decide that I really want to be a lawyer or a scientist or something. It's too early to decide. What about you?"

Karen shrugged. "I guess I'm the same way. I don't even know where I want to go to college yet. But at least you can make some money for college with the band, right?"

"Absolutely," Don said. "I've been saving most of the money I make with the Sevilles for the last year. By the time I start college, I'll have a pretty good amount saved. I plan to play with a band in college and make some money there, too."

"It sounds good to me."

"If it sounds so good to you, why don't you think about doing it yourself? I wasn't kidding, you know. The guys and I have been talking about adding a female singer. And you fit both requirements."

"Both requirements?" asked Karen, puzzled.

Don ticked them off on his fingers. "Number one, you're a female, right? And number two, as it turns out, you're definitely a singer."

"But—"

"And I bet you and I could write a lot of great stuff for the band. If you're going to write songs that we use, then you should be a part of the band and make your fair share of the money."

"I just don't think I can do it. And anyway, I'm not the one you want."

"Why aren't you the one we want?"

"Well...you want someone who's...who's beautiful. Most female singers are."

Don frowned and shook his head. "First of all, the main thing about singers is whether or not they can sing, not how they look. And second, I think you're very pretty."

Karen looked away, blushing. "Oh, come on!"

"No, really. Who says you're not?"

"Nobody *has* to say it. I can just tell." She wanted to leave.

"Well, you're wrong. I think you're pretty."

Karen shook her head. "Guys aren't exactly falling all over me to ask me out."

Don looked thoughtful for a moment. He said, "You know, Karen, *I* think you've *decided* that you're not attractive, and guys can sort of sense that."

"Oh, right. I see. How did you get to be such an expert?"

"I'm not an expert, Karen. But I've spent a lot of time going to hear a lot of singers and hanging around clubs. I've seen singers who look beautiful onstage come out of a dressing room looking like nothing special. But somehow, when they're onstage, they *know* they're looking good. And so do other people. I figure how you *think* you look is as important as how you actually look."

"You really think so?"

"You've got fantastic eyes. And when you were singing before and really *into* it, your eyes lit up. *And you looked beautiful.* And I'm not just saying that to be nice."

Karen spoke so softly it was almost a whisper. "Why *are* you saying it?"

Don studied her for a long moment. Then he stood up and shut off the music. With his attention fixed on the stereo, he said. "Because I want you to think some more about singing with the Sevilles."

"Oh." Karen bit her lip. "But, I'm telling you, I'd get self-conscious on a stage in front of a lot of people. I'd just stand there like a lump."

Don turned around. "I don't think so. Just because you're a little shy around people at school doesn't mean it'll happen onstage. You like singing. I think that once you get into the music, you're going to forget to be shy. And people will get to see you the way *I* saw you tonight.

"Karen, believe me. I wouldn't encourage you if I thought it would be bad for you or the band. Would you be willing to just try one thing? And if it doesn't feel good, then we'll forget about it."

"What?"

"We're rehearsing on Saturday here in the studio. Come over at two and just try singing with the band for a while. If you don't like it, or if I don't like it, or if the band doesn't like it, then okay. That's the end of it. But if we *do* all think that it will work…"

"Then what?"

"Then I want you to think about joining the Sevilles and making your first appearance with us at the Homecoming Dance. Don't say anything about it until you've sung with us Saturday, all right?"

"I…it won't…how…"

"Saturday afternoon. Two o'clock. Hey, I better drive you home. Tomorrow's a school day."

Karen got up to go. She felt a bit dizzy, like she was riding the Hurricane at Playland. She wondered how the ride was going to end.

Chapter Nine

Promptly at two o'clock on Saturday afternoon, Karen walked into the basement studio, where the Sevilles were all at work setting up their equipment and tuning their instruments. Bobby looked up from where he was tightening the screw on a big cymbal and smiled in greeting. "Karen! How you doin'?"

"I'm okay," she answered with a small smile.

Ed was twisting knobs and pushing buttons at the synthesizer. Apparently he always wore dark sunglasses, indoors or out. He glanced over and said, "Hey, man." Everyone, male or female, was "man" to Ed. "You got any more new songs today?"

Karen took some paper from her purse and showed it to him. "Maybe."

"Out of sight! Hey, it's great talking to you, but I gotta do something about this frammistat and set the fubar on the flammerator over here. And somebody's been messing with the goopage readout, so the kannelation is way off. Later."

At least that's what it sounded like to Karen, who just nodded.

The two guitarists, Paul and Fred, also said their hellos. Only the band members were present today. Don was tuning his bass. He'd pluck a string, play a note on the synthesizer, frown, twist a tuning knob, and then try the whole process again. Finally, he was satisfied and put the bass down. He walked over to Karen, who had been standing and watching all the setting up.

"Good to see you. You all ready for this?"

She grinned nervously. "I don't know. I hope so."

"I think you're going to be just fine! We all talked about it earlier, and everybody agreed. If it sounds good, you're in. If it doesn't, then there's no harm done, and no one'll ever know anything about it. Okay?"

"Well... I'll try."

"Karen, listen. It'll be just like it was the other night when it was just me playing. You can sing, and you like to sing. You just wait—it'll feel *right*."

"Okay."

"Here's your mike." Don walked over to a microphone on a stand. "We'll adjust it to your height..." He lowered it about a foot. "That should do it. Okay, now if it feels comfortable, you can leave it like it is, on the stand, but if you want, you can unhook it, like this, if you want to move around." He pulled the mike out of its bracket, showed her how it worked, and then put it back. "Come on over. Is this comfortable?"

She stood in front of the mike. "How close should I be?"

"You can get up real close. That's right. That way, you can sing soft and the mike will pick up your voice. But if you want to really sing out, you should back off a bit. You'll get the idea soon enough."

91

She nodded again, and waited in front of the mike.

Don looked at the rest of the band. "Everybody ready? All tuned up? Okay, let's try 'The Difference.' Karen, do you remember your words, or do you need to have them in front of you?"

"I remember."

"Good. Now, there's an intro on lead guitar, and then we come in. Just like last week. Okay? Right! One. Two. One, two, three, four..."

Fred's guitar hit the opening, the rest of the band came in, but Karen stood there silent.

Don waved the band to a stop. "Is there a problem?"

"No, I...no. I just...could you start again?"

The band started again, and this time Karen began to sing:

"What's the difference
What clothes I choose to wear,
How I want to keep my hair..."

It was a surprise to her at first when her voice came out of a speaker, amplified just like the instruments. But she was singing the right notes, and staying in rhythm with the band. In fact, she didn't sound bad at all. She looked around at Don, who gave her a smile of encouragement. He was swaying as he plucked the bass line, enjoying the music—singing and all.

Karen forgot her self-consciousness within a couple of verses. She let the emotions of the song take over. Her voice rose in volume and there was a shrill electronic howl from the speakers. Without thinking about it, she backed off from the mike stand and the howl went away.

To her additional surprise, she discovered that she was moving with the music, something she usually had a hard time doing in front of other people. When she moved, the distance between her and the mike varied, so she pulled the microphone out of its bracket and held it so that she could sing and move and keep her volume steady.

When the song ended, the band was silent for a moment. The silence was broken by a clash of cymbals. "All *ri-i-i-ight*!" Bobby exclaimed.

Paul, the rhythm guitarist, said, "Hey, Karen, come on! You telling us that this is the first time you ever sang with a band? Unbe*leee*vable!"

"Like, she's *got* it, man," said Ed, who almost smiled behind his shades.

And Karen blushed, but for once she was blushing in sheer pleasure.

But Don was all business. "Let's run through it again," he said. "This time, Karen, keep it quiet at first, and let it build. Let's put in a solo for Ed after the third verse, and one for Fingers after the fourth, and then let it all out for the last verse. Also, Karen, don't be surprised—we'll be singing harmony behind you this time. Just go right on doing your thing, okay? Let's go!"

The second time through, Don, Paul, and Fred sang a backup harmony, and the blend of voices sent a thrill right through Karen's bones.

They then tried some other songs from the Sevilles' book, some oldies that Karen knew the words to, as well as some more recent hits. She and Don sang one as a vocal duet. She found that she was able to sing a harmony line with the other band members. It just seemed natural to her.

When Don finally said, "Let's take a break," she was astonished to find out that over two hours had gone by. Bobby trotted upstairs and came back with a trayful of soft drinks and a batch of cookies. Everyone grabbed snacks and wolfed them down.

"Karen's got a new song called 'Attraction' that I wrote some music for," announced Don. "Let's try it after the break. I think she and I can alternate verses, and then do a two-part harmony on the last verse. Okay with you, Karen?"

"Sure."

"You have more new stuff?" asked Ed. Karen showed him a sheaf of paper, with words to three possible songs on it. "Two are poems I wrote last year that would make good lyrics, and *this* one I wrote yesterday."

Ed glanced through them all, and then went back and looked over one of them more closely. He tapped Don on the shoulder. "Hey, dude, can I have a shot at writing music for this one? I dig it; it has real soul."

Don shrugged. "Why not? She writes faster than I can keep up with by myself."

Fred shoved his baseball cap back on his head and drained his root beer off. "Say, Karen, you were really *cookin'* there. Looks like you're a singer after all."

"Thanks. It was fun."

"So...when are you going to start doing gigs with us?"

"Gigs? Oh, I don't know...I wasn't thinking about...you really mean performing with you?"

"Sure," Fred replied. "That's what this is all about, isn't it? To see if you could work with us or not?"

"I know that's what Don said, but I'm not sure if I *can*."

"Of course you can," insisted Fred. "You're a natural." He turned to the other Sevilles for approval. "Isn't that right, guys?"

There was general agreement from the group. Everyone seemed to want to talk at once. They assured Karen that she was a welcome addition to the band. Don waved his arms to get the attention of the other musicians.

"Let's sit down in the den and talk this out for a bit before we go back to work."

They trooped out of the studio and sat down in the next room. Karen sat in one of the comfortable old armchairs. Don pulled a folding chair from the studio in front of the stereo and sat facing the others.

"The guys have talked about this a lot lately. We all decided that if you were able to do a good job singing with us, that we would ask you to join the Sevilles. We could use another lead singer, especially one who writes. And after hearing you today, I guess I can make it official." He looked around at the others, who all seemed to feel the same way. "We want you in, and we figure that a good time to introduce you as the newest Seville would be the Hampstead High Homecoming Dance. That'd give us four weekends to rehearse. As far as money goes, we've always split what we earn equally, and we'd do the same thing now, just that we'd be cutting it up six ways instead of five."

Paul jumped in. "But we figure that we'll be

doing more work with you in the band, so we'll do as well or better than we have been doing."

Karen still didn't appear too happy.

"Is there a problem for you?" asked Don. "If you have any questions, or want to talk about something, this'd be a good time for it."

Karen sighed and leaned forward, trying to find the right words.

"I really enjoy singing with the Sevilles. You guys are great, really. But singing in the studio with no one else around to watch is one thing, performing in front of an audience is something I'm not sure I can handle..." She faltered and stopped.

"What you're saying," said Don, "is that you're shy in front of people. Right?"

Karen nodded.

"So what else is new?" said Ed. "I feel the same way with people. Why do you think I wear these things all the time?" He took off his sunglasses and gestured with them. "They're, like, my mask. When I don't have 'em on, I feel freaky. Even with *these* guys. And I've been playing with them for two years now."

"You sure don't look shy while you're singing," Fred put in.

"And you should remember," added Don, "that it wouldn't just be Karen Gillespie up there in front of people. It'd be the *Sevilles*."

"The coolest, hippest, funkiest band in the city!" said Ed.

"In the *state*!" said Paul.

"In the en-tire country!" proclaimed Bobby, and everybody broke up in laughter.

Karen couldn't help joining in the laughs.

Finally, she stood up and said, "You guys are terrific, and I'm happy that you want to work with me. I'd like to think about it for a while, if that's all right."

"Take your time," replied Don. "If you want to talk some more later on, that's cool. But you know how we feel about you. Now, let's get to work on that new song."

As they filed back into the studio, Karen found herself thinking about what Don had said. "You know how *we* feel about you." What she really wanted to know, but couldn't possibly bring herself to ask, was how did *he* feel about her? Was he interested in her only as a writer and singer? Or was there something more?

The song "Attraction" came together smoothly, even faster than "The Difference" had the week before. Karen and Don sang alternating verses, and then sang the last verse together in close harmony. As they sang, they leaned in to the same mike, so that their faces were only inches apart. Karen was suddenly aware of the lyrics more strongly than ever:

> "Like a magnet does to steel,
>   Like a flower does to a bee,
>   Like catnip does to kittens, babe,
>   That's what you do to me,
>   It's called attraction..."

Was she feeling that kind of attraction toward Don? It sure seemed like it. And what if he only wanted to be a friend and working partner? Would she be able to stand being around him, singing with him, if he was going with another girl? That was something to think about.

The rehearsal went on for another hour, and by that time, six songs in addition to her own two had been set aside as vocals for Karen. The other members of the band were packing up their gear when Don asked her, "Can you stick around for a little while? I'd like to talk to you some more, if you don't mind."

"Sure."

"Great! I'll be right back." Don went over to help Bobby carry out his drum kit. As the Sevilles climbed the stairs out of the basement, loaded down with instruments and amps, they all said friendly goodbyes to Karen. Ed, who was taking a couple of Bobby's cymbals, stopped and turned back.

"I just wanted to say...like, I really hope you work with us. See you." She was left alone in the silent studio.

She walked around, stopping to look over some of the sheets of music Don had written, which were nothing but scribbling to her. She sat in one of the folding chairs and tried to settle her mind, which seemed to be spinning around, full of confusing questions and doubts. She felt that the notions she'd had of herself—who she was and what she could do—were changing so fast that she wasn't able to keep up. A dream she had had might be coming true, and now another dream was teasing her, one that appeared too good to ever come true. Could it ever happen that Don...

Don walked back into the studio, ending her daydreaming. He didn't say anything at first, but paced around as if he was nervous about something.

"Can I get you anything? Something to drink? A snack?"

"No, thanks. I'm fine."

"Well, what do you say we go in the next room, where it's more comfortable?"

They sat down in the den, Karen on the faded couch and Don in an armchair. Don ran his fingers through his mop of light brown hair, then leaned forward toward her.

"You know, up until this session today, I wasn't certain that you could be a part of the Sevilles. But now it's as if it was meant to be. You sound like you've been doing this for years, the stuff you write is wonderful, and the guys like you."

She smiled at him, feeling her eyes lock with his bright blue ones. "Well...I like the guys. And I had a lot of fun today."

"That's great! So, is there anything else on your mind, anything worrying you about being a part of the Sevilles?"

"I just don't know about getting up in front of a crowd of people. It scares me."

"I understand. But, remember, you were real nervous about singing with nobody around but me, and you got over it right away. Then you were scared about singing with the band—I could tell when you first got in front of the microphone. But you got over *that* in five minutes, and there wasn't any problem."

"Yes, but..."

"Karen, you're good at making music, and you *like* making music. I know, because I feel the same way. And when you're doing it, there's no room left in your mind to worry about what people are thinking about *you*. I'll bet the same thing'll happen when you're in front of an audience. You'll forget that they're there. And they'll *love* you."

She gave him a long, thoughtful look. "You really think so?"

"Absolutely. I'm positive."

Karen let out a long sigh. "I don't know... things are happening so fast. It's so confusing. Secretly I've always wanted to be a singer, ever since I was little. But it was just make-believe, like wanting to be a princess, or to go to Never-Never Land with Peter Pan. And now you're telling me it isn't a dream anymore."

"It doesn't have to be. You can make this one happen, if you're willing to trust me, and take your shot."

"Well...if you think it's possible..."

"I do."

"And the band really wants me..."

"They already said so."

"Then I guess I'll go for it."

"That's great!" Don jumped up and reached out to grab Karen by both hands. He pulled her out of her chair and spun her around, whooping and laughing. When they came to a stop, he pressed her hands.

"You won't be sorry, I promise."

Karen smiled. "I'd like to ask one favor."

"What?"

"I'd rather keep it a secret until the night of the dance. Would that be all right?"

He gave her a puzzled look as he let go of her hands. "Sure, I guess so. Why?"

"Just so I won't be bothered about it. I'm scared enough as it is."

"That's okay. For the next few weeks, you're going to be so busy you won't have time to feel scared."

"Busy doing what?"

Don began ticking off points on his fingers. "Rehearsing. Shopping for outfits to wear onstage. Writing at least a couple of new songs. Getting new band photos, with you in them. Figuring out a new look for your hair. That's just for starters."

She took a deep breath. "Plus, of course, going to school and eating and sleeping and stuff like that."

Don shrugged. "I never said changing your life was going to be easy. But it'll sure be interesting."

Chapter Ten

The time began to fly by—Karen felt like the days were all melting together. The Sevilles upped their rehearsal schedule to two weekday evenings plus Saturdays, to work her into the group and learn more material. Also, she met one evening a week with Don to start learning how to read music.

On the nights when she wasn't rehearsing, she whipped through her homework in order to have time to work on new lyrics. She'd go over the songs she was to sing in her head, again and again. She began to dream about them.

She had told only three people her secret, and all three were pledged to silence. Two were her parents, who seemed pleased at seeing Karen so active and eager, but puzzled at the notion of their quiet daughter being a rock singer.

The third one was Gwen. Karen felt a little awkward about Gwen, because there never seemed to be time for the two to get together. They'd see each other in the halls or the cafeteria at school. But she'd only have enough time for a few words. When Gwen called to suggest getting together for an evening, Karen would have to put her off. She simply had no spare time.

After two and a half weeks of the mad scramble, when only two weeks remained before the Homecoming Dance, she bumped into Gwen—literally bumped into her—between classes.

"Sorry! Hi, Gwen."

"Hello there, stranger! You look just like a girl I used to know, a long, long time ago. We used to be good friends. I wonder whatever happened to her?" Gwen was smiling, but there was a hurt look in her eyes.

Karen suddenly felt ashamed. "I know, I've been terrible! It's just that I've been running around so much...how about meeting me for lunch later? There's a lot to tell you."

Gwen tilted her head and studied her friend. "Sure you have the time? I don't want to get in the way."

"Gwen, I'm really sorry. I didn't mean to cut you off like this, it just happened. I'll fill you in at lunch, okay?"

"Well, all right, I'll save you a seat. Bye."

"I've got to run. I'll be late for English. Bye."

At lunchtime, Karen actually beat Gwen to the cafeteria and grabbed two chairs for them. She had only a container of skim milk and an apple. When Gwen appeared a moment later, carrying a tray, she waved her over.

Gwen set her tray down, staring at Karen. "You know, I think this is the first time you've beat me here all year."

"I guess I've gotten into the habit of rushing everywhere lately."

Gwen inspected Karen closely. "Have you lost weight?"

"I think so, maybe five pounds. I just use more energy. Those rehearsals can be exhausting."

"It looks good on you. You have cheekbones. I never realized that."

"It does? Oh, great! I needed to hear that! I've got to buy something to wear for the dance, and I don't have the slightest idea what I should get. I need some advice—about hair, too. Are you available?"

"Sure! Especially since it might be the last chance I·have to spend time with you for a while."

"Oh, thanks! We'll talk about when's a good time to shop. Where's Phil? How are things between you two?"

Gwen frowned. "Okay, I guess, except now that basketball practice has started, I don't see much of him, either. He's at practice after school every day, and then he's got to get home right away and eat and do homework. Lunch hour, he does laps and stuff because he says he's out of shape.

"So we only see each other weekends, and basically that's just on Saturday nights. And once the basketball *season* starts, there'll be games on Saturdays, and we may *never* see each other—until March anyway."

She sighed, and gave Karen a gloomy look. "I wish I was in your shoes—I mean, you won't just be seeing your boyfriend, you're going to be working with him, and you'll be making money while you do."

"Gwen, will you please stop? He's *not* my boyfriend! He hasn't done anything or said anything to show he wants me as a girlfriend."

"Well, what about you? Have you said anything to *him*?"

"No."

"Why not? I think I know how you feel about him."

"Oh, Gwen...I can't...what if he's really only interested in working with me, and nothing else? It could ruin everything. I want this to work, Gwen. I want my dream to come true. Half the time, I feel sure that it will, and that I'll make it as a singer. The rest of the time, I get scared to death that it won't, and that I'll look ridiculous and so will Don and the band...I *couldn't* say anything to him, not now."

"Karen?" came a voice from across the table. The two girls looked up to see Jennifer McSwain standing there, with a nervous grin. "Can I talk to you for a second?"

Karen stared at Jennifer in surprise, then said, "I guess so." There was an empty chair across from the two friends. Jennifer took it.

"I wanted to say that I'm awfully sorry about what happened at that band rehearsal. It was all my fault. Donny told me how upset I got you."

"I'll say," muttered Gwen, and Karen poked her in the ribs.

"That's okay," Karen replied. "I overreacted."

"I was just so *jealous* of you," Jennifer went on. "I was hoping that Donny would want to go steady with me, and there he was, paying all that attention to you, and...I acted pretty horrible, and I hope you forgive me."

"Uh...sure, I'm glad you came over. I know it wasn't easy."

Jennifer looked anxiously at Gwen, who had an unfriendly frown on her face. "You too, Gwen. I've felt so embarrassed about it, and I want to get it off my mind."

"Well..." Gwen's frown softened into a smile. "I guess I understand how you felt. When Phil was going with Jeannie Fox, I used to think I *hated* her, and I hardly even knew her."

Jennifer shook her head. "It's funny how you can dislike someone you don't really know. I always thought you were such a snob, Karen. But Donny said that wasn't true, it only looked that way because you're shy around other people. So... well, I wanted to just apologize."

"So, have you given up on Donny—uh, Don?" asked Gwen.

Jennifer nodded sadly. "He says he likes me as a friend, but that's all."

Gwen suddenly sat up straight, and turned to Karen with a gleam in her eye. "I just had a *brilliant* idea! You want to get advice about changing your hairstyle, right? Well, who knows more about that stuff than..." She motioned toward Jennifer.

Karen decided to take the plunge. She leaned across to Jennifer. "If you can keep a secret, I have a favor to ask."

"Sure. What is it?"

Karen stood up. "Let's go out in the hall, where it's more private."

The three girls walked out of the cafeteria and found a quiet corner. Karen turned to face Jennifer.

"First, here's the secret. I'm going to start singing with the Sevilles, beginning with the Homecoming Dance."

Jennifer's eyes widened. "That's...that's wonderful. You know, I really liked the song you wrote with Donny. But I didn't know you sang."

"Me neither, until two weeks ago...but that's another story. The thing is...I have to get myself all fixed up for the dance. I need something special to wear, and I have to do something to my hair but I don't really know anything about fashion and hairstyles—I never paid much attention to that stuff before...."

Gwen cut in. "She wanted me to give her some tips, but I figure *you're* the real expert here."

"So," Karen picked up, "do you think you can give me some ideas? I'd really be grateful."

Jennifer stepped back a little and gave Karen a once-over. Then she smiled. "Sure, I can give you ideas, if you think they'll help. I tell you what, why don't you and Gwen and I get together after school one day this week? I'll bring some magazines, and we can look at the pictures and decide what would look best for you. How does that sound?"

"Oh, that would be wonderful," said Karen. "I can't tonight, there's a rehearsal, but how about tomorrow?"

"Fine!" said Jennifer. "I can come over to your place. Gwen, can you be there too?"

"Well, Phil has basketball practice, but...do you really want *me* there? I wouldn't get in the way?"

"In the way? Of course not," Karen answered. "It'll be like a group decision. It'll be fun!"

"Well, all right. Seven-thirty at your house. I'll bring some munchies!"

Just after seven-thirty the following evening, the three girls were up in Karen's bedroom, with magazines spread all over the bed. Jennifer had arrived lugging a stack of some of the latest fashion magazines. She had also brought a large vanity case, which turned out to be full of all kinds of makeup. "We can try a few things out," she explained.

Gwen picked up a picture of a dark-haired model whose hair was cut very short and spiky in front. "What do you think of this?"

Jennifer gave it a little thought, but Karen shook her head. "It wouldn't feel right. It's just not *me*, somehow."

Karen liked another picture, where the girl's hair was cut straight across the forehead and bobbed in the back. But Jennifer didn't think it would work. "It'd get in the way of your eyes too much. We want those to really come out, because you've got such fabulous eyes."

"Really?" asked Karen in surprise.

"I'd give anything for eyes like yours," said Jennifer. "Mine are small and squinty."

"No, they're not," protested Gwen.

"Well, anyway, they're not as big and beautiful as Karen's. We want to highlight them."

Jennifer picked up another magazine and leafed through it, and then abruptly stopped. "How about something like this?" She held a picture out to the others. The girl in it wore her hair in really tight curls.

"A body wave?" Karen sounded doubtful. "Do you really think that would work?"

Jennifer gave Karen a thoughtful examination. "I think so. Especially if we...let's try something with the makeup." She delved into her vanity case.

For about ten minutes, Karen sat in her desk chair, lit by the two lamps in her room, while Jennifer worked on her with brushes, eye liner, rouge, and something she called "highlighter," which she applied to Karen's cheekbones. Jennifer explained what she was doing as she did it, adding, "Now this may seem a little too heavy, but remember, you'll be on a stage under bright lights. Let's just underline the eyes—this is fun!—and some powder...okay, take a look."

Gwen let out a soft, admiring "Wow," as Karen took the hand mirror that Jennifer offered her.

It was startling. Karen put on makeup so rarely herself that she'd never developed a knack for it, and it tended to look strange to her eyes. But Jennifer clearly knew what she was doing, and the face that looked back at her from the mirror was... well, *different*, but *appealing*. It looked good. Correction: *She* looked good. She found it hard to take her eyes off the mirror, but finally she broke away from it and said to Jennifer, "You're a genius. I don't know what to say."

"I'm not a genius. I can just see your good features better than you can." Quickly, Jennifer showed Karen exactly what she had done, and wrote a short list of makeup supplies that Karen would need to do it herself.

"And you think a permanent would work for me?"

"Your hair's straight, but it has body. I think it'd be fantastic with this look. It'll set off those eyes."

Karen turned to Gwen, who held up her hands. "Don't look at *me*! After the change Jennifer just made in the way you look, I'd say just follow her lead. Go for the permanent."

Karen took another look in the mirror and felt light-headed and excited. "Okay! I'll get it next week."

"Great!" Jennifer appeared to have caught Karen's feeling of eagerness. "You know, there's a salon in the Downtown Mall where they'll do a wonderful job for you. And there are a couple of boutiques where you can probably find something really perfect for your outfit. I'll go with you, if you want."

"Oh, that'd be great! I'm so grateful for what you're doing."

Jennifer shrugged it off. "Listen, I'm always looking for an excuse to do some shopping. Let's pick a day after school next week, and we can *all* go."

Karen looked once more at her new face in the mirror.

Gwen poked her in the shoulder. "If you and your mirror would rather be alone, Jennifer and I can just leave."

Karen laughed and put the mirror down. "It's just so...I didn't expect...I can't get over the difference. Let's see what there is to drink in the refrigerator that goes with the junk food that Gwen brought."

Eight days later, the band met for a Saturday afternoon rehearsal. There was one week left until the Homecoming Dance. The day before, Karen, Gwen, and Jennifer had gone over to the Downtown Mall and Karen had had her hair done while the other girls window-shopped and checked out the action. They returned to the salon later, just as Karen was coming out from under a hairdryer. Even Jennifer was amazed at the transformation. The rich brown curls framed a truly pretty face.

Karen had put on makeup as Jennifer had shown her, and the three girls went to find a performance outfit for Karen. They'd settled on two: a sleeveless, short black dress with a mock turtleneck; and a red jumpsuit with a cinched waist. Unable to make up her mind between the two, Karen decided to see if the other Sevilles had a preference. As they left the mall, some of the local guys hanging around whistled and made approving remarks about them. Karen was startled, and then pleased, to realize that the remarks were meant as much for her as for her friends.

Now, Don's sister, Linda, let her into the house. Linda stepped back and stared in open admiration as Karen took off her jacket to reveal the black dress.

"Gee, you look beautiful!"

Karen smiled at the girl. "You think so?"

"I sure do!"

Encouraged, carrying the jumpsuit, Karen went downstairs to the basement and opened the studio door.

As usual, the five musicians were busily involved in getting their gear set up and organized, and at first were too preoccupied to look at her. But then Ed looked up and did a double take. His lower jaw dropped open; he seemed unable to say anything.

Bobby saw her as he tightened a bolt on a cymbal. He straightened up, and finally said, "Awesome!"

The other Sevilles stopped what they were doing, and all of them gazed at her, dazzled. Don was the last to notice, and he broke into a huge smile.

"Karen! You...you look...fantastic!"

Karen twirled around to show off the dress. "Thanks! I brought this other outfit along, in case you want to check it out, but..."

"No, no!" Don slowly walked over, his eyes staying fixed on her. "I mean, maybe for another gig, but you look fantastic like this. I mean, I knew you were pretty, but this..."

"Well, I have to give a lot of the credit to Jennifer."

"Jennifer?" Don was startled. "Jennifer McSwain?"

Karen nodded. "You were right about her, Don. She really can be sweet. She helped me out with choosing clothes, and with my hair and makeup. Does everybody approve?"

There followed a loud chorus of approval from five impressed males. Don stood in front of her, seemingly unable to think of anything at all to say. It was Karen who broke the silence. "Well, what do you say we get to work here?"

They ran through all the material that featured Karen—twelve songs, which included four originals, with her lyrics and Don's music. They rehearsed some numbers that Don sang, as well as some instrumentals. For a few of these, Karen played rhythm instruments, like a tambourine or the maracas, which she'd found easy to master.

At four o'clock, they wrapped up for the day.

As they packed their equipment up, the guys kept looking over at Karen, as if they couldn't get over the change in her appearance. When they hauled their cases and boxes upstairs, she stayed behind.

Don came back down the stairs after helping with the gear, and stopped when he saw Karen. He appeared to be uncomfortable, shuffling sheets of music and walking around the room, saying nothing for a few minutes. Karen watched him, puzzled.

Finally, he turned to her. "Well...good work today. I guess I'll see you Wednesday night, for the last meeting before the gig."

He sounded cold and impersonal to Karen, as if he were speaking to a casual acquaintance.

"Don? Is everything all right?"

"All right? Sure. Why do you ask?"

She started to run her fingers through her hair, an old habit she resorted to when she was trying to think, but when she felt the tight curls, she pulled her hand away.

"I don't know. You seem...kind of different. Are you...angry or something? Is there anything the matter?"

He didn't look directly at her. "Of course nothing's the matter. We had a good rehearsal, you look fantastic, and we're all set for the dance. What could be the matter?"

"Well, I just thought..."

"Listen, Karen, I've got a lot to do today, so I better get at it. Can I give you a lift home?"

Something was obviously bugging him, but she couldn't figure it out. "No, that's okay, I can walk. See you, Don."

"Bye."

Still wondering what had happened to make him turn unfriendly, she went unhappily upstairs and left, waving goodbye to Mrs. Stanton, who was planting bulbs in the flowerbeds in the front yard.

During the following week, she saw Don occasionally, but he never did more than nod to her or exchange brief and impersonal hellos. At the same time, other guys in her classes began conversations with her for the very first time. One of them, a tall, good-looking football player named Randy Marshall, who had never spoken to her before, asked her if she had plans for the dance that weekend.

She told him she was busy. He looked disappointed.

On Friday she had lunch with Gwen, who had resisted all temptation to share Karen's big secret with anyone, including Phil. She and Phil were, of course, going to the dance.

Gwen nibbled on a green salad. "Am I imagining things," she said, "or are a lot of guys hitting on you lately?"

"Well...I guess some of them are treating me like I'm a new girl in school, someone they've never seen before. It's a little weird. I even got asked to the dance by Randy Marshall, and he never even talked to me once before this week."

"You better get used to it." Gwen pushed away her salad. "Jennifer has changed your life, Karen."

Karen didn't look all that happy about it. "I just wish I could figure out what's happened to Don. Ever since he saw me in my 'new look,' he's been treating me like a stranger. I don't know what's going on with him."

Gwen thought for a moment. "Maybe there's something on his mind, something at home you don't know anything about. Or maybe he's getting real nervous about the dance, and how the band is going to sound. I wouldn't worry about it too much."

Karen nodded unhappily. "Well, I wish I knew what's wrong. I feel like I've done something, but I don't know what it is."

"It'll all work out. You'll see."

The Homecoming Dance was the biggest event of the fall social calendar at Hampstead High. Squads of students had worked long and hard in an effort to transform the gym into a festive ballroom. The lighting was soft, and came mostly from colorful Japanese paper lamps with low-level light bulbs inside. Lengths of red and white material had been hung to mask the basketball backboards and other gym equipment, and a stage was set up at one end of the room for the band. The stage was framed by more red and white cloth, and some black curtains, to give the band an off-stage area to rest, and to turn one of the gym entrances into a "stage door" so that they could come and go without having to fight through the crowd.

At seven-thirty, the Sevilles were setting up. The dance was due to start at eight. Karen, who had almost no setting up to do, was pacing nervously backstage. There had been no exchanges between her and Don, except what was necessary for work.

She felt all of the old fears coming back to her as the clock crept closer to the fatal hour of eight. For one panicky second, she thought of rushing up to Don and saying, "Let's forget the whole thing, I simply can't do it"—and then pushed the thought out of her mind.

"Karen! Where *is* she, anyway?" The sound of Don's irritated voice brought her out on the stage, where he stood with his bass slung over his shoulders, ready to go, as was the rest of the band.

"I'm right here," she said.

"Well, don't wander away like that! We've got things to do here!"

"I was just—"

"Oh, never mind. Let's run a sound check. Let's try 'The Difference,' okay? One. Two. One, two, three, four..."

When Karen started her vocal, there was a loud electronic screech from the speakers. Don waved his arm to stop the song.

"Hold it, hold it! Karen, that mike is set way too loud! Didn't you check it while we were setting up?"

"Check it? I didn't know—"

"Karen, you're working with us now, you have to pay attention and do your job. There's no time for daydreaming." Don made some adjustments on a control panel.

"Hey, Don, chill out," said Paul. "She's never done this stuff before, right? Let's not get crazy now, okay?"

Don nodded. "Okay, okay, sorry. Let's take it again." He counted the beat off, and they started the song again. This time, everything sounded right. Nobody was in the gym yet, except for a few kids getting the refreshments ready. Karen couldn't tell whether they had liked what they'd heard.

"Right," said Don. "Let's leave everything set up here and go backstage and go over the order we're going to play everything."

Everyone filed off the bandstand. Karen felt numb. She couldn't understand what was going on with Don, but she was far too worried about her public debut as a singer to let anything else bother her.

After they had gone over the order in which they were going to play their numbers, the members of the band had ten minutes to relax. One after another, they came up to Karen and wished her good luck. Working with them in rehearsals had made her feel close to all of them, she realized, and she felt how much they wanted her to make a big hit tonight. Don was the last one to approach her, and his "Good luck" was very mechanical and cool.

A girl from the dance committee peered backstage and announced, "It's eight o'clock. We're opening the doors."

Karen could hear a confused mix of voices as the people streamed in. The plan was for the original five Sevilles to come on first, and do a couple of numbers. Then Don would introduce her from the stage.

"Okay, guys," he said. "Let's get out there." They filed out to their positions, and the crowd noise got suddenly louder. Karen felt her heart pounding, and she concentrated on breathing slowly and regularly.

She could hear Don counting off the first song of the evening, and the band began to play. It sounded strange and echoey when she listened from backstage. She went over to the curtains that separated her from the crowd and peeked through. It looked like there were hundreds of kids already on their feet, dancing and milling around. She thought that she'd spotted Gwen and Phil, but she couldn't be sure. *Breathe slowly,* she told herself. *Don't panic. You know what you have to do.*

The band went through several songs, as planned. Then the music stopped, and Karen heard Don's amplified voice.

"Good evening, everybody. We're gonna have a rockin' time tonight." There was cheering and whistling from the crowd. "But right now," he went on, "we have a very special surprise for you all." The crowd noise hushed noticeably. "Tonight, we will be introducing to you for the first time a new member of the Sevilles. She's pretty and talented, and she can really sing. She writes some great songs, and we'll be doing some of them tonight. Some of you already know her, but tonight you're gonna see and hear a really special girl, like she's never been seen before. Let's have a big, welcoming hand for the newest Seville—Karen Gillespie!"

Bobby did a drum roll and a cymbal clash, and Karen walked onstage into a glare of light and a blare of sound. She took deep, slow breaths as she reached the microphone and unclipped it from its stand. Then she looked back at Don and nodded. Don counted off and the band went into "The Difference." As the music began, Karen suddenly felt the nervousness drop away. The lights and strange loud noise didn't matter anymore—only the music. She picked up the mike and sang:

>   "What's the difference
>   What clothes I choose to wear,
>   How I want to keep my hair..."

just as they'd been rehearsing it, with instrumental solos and then a big stormy climax. As the number went on, she was dimly aware that a lot of kids who had been dancing had stopped and were moving closer to the stage, just to listen.

The song reached the end, and there was a silence that lasted for maybe two seconds. Then an explosion of yells, cheers, whistles, and applause filled the room. Karen stood there, looking down, barely able to take it in. She saw Gwen with Phil, both of them jumping up and down, yelling something that couldn't be heard over the general uproar. Jennifer McSwain and her date were cheering and clapping frantically. It was a couple of minutes before the group was able to get on with the next number.

The next forty-five minutes went by like a dream. She sang and played her maracas and tambourine, and whether the huge mob of kids was dancing or just listening to her, she felt that there was something between them—that they were focused on her, that they *enjoyed* her, that they wanted *more*... that her dream had become a reality.

At the end of their first set, Don announced to the densely packed room, "We're going to take fifteen minutes, and then we'll be back with a lot more of the same, so cool out and rest up. See you!"

There was more yelling and cheering, and then a steady, rhythmic handclapping as the Sevilles left the stage.

Once behind the curtains, Karen was mobbed by the others in the group, all of them hugging her, whooping and hollering, saying how fantastic she had been, that never in their work together had there been any evening like it...all except Don, whom Karen saw slip out the stage door, which led out to a grassy plot alongside the gym.

She said, "Excuse me, guys, but I'm going to get some air," and went out through the same door. She looked around for Don and saw him leaning up against the school wall, looking out at nothing in particular.

She walked up to him, and quietly said, "Don? It's going pretty well, isn't it?"

"Yeah." He looked straight ahead and said nothing more.

Karen couldn't stand his silence any longer.

"Don, what is it? What's the matter? I don't understand—have I done something that you're angry about? Why won't you *talk* to me?"

He gave her a flat, cool look. "I talk to you. I'm talking to you now, right?"

"Not *really* talking, Don. Ever since I came to that rehearsal last Saturday, it's been awful—you've been acting like you hardly know me. Don't you like the way I look now? Because if you don't I'll change it. But please, don't shut me out like this."

He stared at her and laughed, but not happily. "Not like the way you look? Karen, you're *beautiful.* I knew you'd look good, but I had no *idea* what... no, you shouldn't change anything about yourself."

"Then what...*please* tell me." She drew closer to him.

He studied her for a moment, and then gave her

a wry grin. "Well, why not?" He took a deep, ragged breath.

"Ever since I first met you, I just felt something about you…was special to me. Maybe it's your eyes, I don't know…I really wanted to see you, go out with you…but I always felt, I don't know, uncomfortable around you."

"Don…"

"No, wait. Let me finish. You're not like the other girls at school, Karen. You didn't fall all over me, or 'yes' me to death…you told me what you really thought. I respected that—but it also scared me a little. Because you were right about my lyrics…I'm not the artist with words that you are. And I thought, 'This girl is different. And she's definitely not interested in me.'

"And then there was that dance, where I acted like a total idiot with you. If you only knew how bad I felt, how much I wanted to do that whole evening over again…. Then things started getting better, we started being friends, and I thought, maybe, just maybe, I can get her to *like* me, to feel something for me like I feel for *her*…

"And then you came into that rehearsal, and you weren't just pretty anymore, you were *beautiful*. I figured, 'Well, that's that. Now every guy in school is going to be hanging around her, and she'll have her pick.' It's not like I'm the only one who can see what you really are anymore, Karen. So, I figure, I've got to get used to the notion of your going out with other guys. That's all."

"That's not so," she said softly, stepping up so that she stood only a foot away from him. "It may be true that a lot of other boys are noticing me now.

But there's only one guy I *want* to notice me. There's only one guy I want to look beautiful for."

He looked into her eyes, not yet ready to believe what she seemed to be saying. "You mean, you... you actually feel..."

She took his hands in hers. "I couldn't bring myself to talk to you like this before, because I thought you just wanted me for a friend. And I was afraid that telling you how I felt would just make it hard for us to work together. So I didn't say anything. But *you're* the one who matters to me, Don."

He put his hands on her shoulders and gently pulled her close to him. Their lips met in a soft, warm kiss.

They broke apart and smiled at one another, holding each other's hands.

"I guess we better not kiss any more," he said. "It'll mess up your makeup."

She squeezed his hands. "Let's go back inside. The other guys will be wondering what's happened to us."

Hand in hand, they walked slowly back to the stage door, where hundreds of dancers waited for them to make more music.